Her heart skipped a beat when Alex leaned into the microphone and thanked the band. His baritone voice sounded even sexier reverberating through the small room.

Cara watched in amusement as a small crowd immediately gathered around the stage. Many were women, both young and old, with cameras in their hands, primping and waiting for the perfect photo opportunity. Over the next few minutes Alex posed for every picture and signed every autograph.

If this was what it was like to be famous, she'd pass. She was glad the only notoriety she'd ever have was the full-page ad for Beacon House in the yellow pages.

Cara straightened as Alex slid into the booth next to her.

"Why didn't you warn me about the groupies? I am seething with jealousy over here."

He draped his arm around the back of the booth, and she unconsciously inched closer to him. "There's no competition here." He twisted a lock of her hair around his finger and tugged on it playfully. "You're still my biggest fan, right?"

She lifted her eyes to his and nodded, wishing that he knew, that she had the courage to tell him, just how much of a fan she was.

He laid his hand against her cheek, and she felt his warm breath on her lips. "And I'm yours."

Their lips melted together in quiet intensity, and everything else—their fear, their pasts and their uncertain future—disappear

Books by Harmony Evans

Harlequin Kimani Romance

Lesson in Romance

HARMONY EVANS

writes sexy, emotional contemporary love stories for women. A former jazz/classical pianist and radio announcer, she is currently a single mom with an overactive imagination still searching for her own happily-ever-after. For more love stories that last a lifetime, visit www.harmonyevans.com or follow @harmonyannevans.

Lesson in
ROMANCE

HARMONY EVANS

HARLEQUIN®
entertain, enrich, inspire™

To my beautiful daughter Angelina,
my first and dearest fan.

Recycling programs
for this product may
not exist in your area.

ISBN-13: 978-0-373-86279-5

LESSON IN ROMANCE

Dear Reader,

What if you couldn't read the words on this page, a letter from your child or husband, or a menu? Those are the sobering questions I asked myself one day and what drove me to write *Lesson in Romance,* my debut novel.

I am always crushing on hot jazz musicians, so Alex is the culmination of my dreams. Although he can't read, the notes he plays on his saxophone and the touch of his hands speak only pleasure. His sexy looks and vulnerability are irresistible to Cara, who's on a mission to help end illiteracy in her Harlem community. Along with the ABC's, she's teaching Alex how to trust and love again. The secrets and experiences they share along the way will change their lives forever.

How has the gift of love and reading affected your life? Please share your thoughts with me at harmonyevans@roadrunner.com!

Be blessed,

Harmony Evans

I'd like to thank Nancy Oakley, Founder,
Project Learn, for her time and patience
in answering my endless questions about tutoring
adult nonreaders and the issues surrounding illiteracy.
Thanks to Mom and Dad, for loving me and
teaching me how to read. Finally, thanks to
Michelle Tackla-Wallace, for believing in me.

Chapter 1

Cara stepped out of the taxi on West 135th Street in Harlem clutching her briefcase like a life preserver, her eyes fixed on the building before her. The growling sounds of a saxophone poured out through an open window belonging to Alex Dovington, a man she'd wanted to meet for nearly thirteen years.

And the same man she had to teach how to read… in three days.

A cramp gripped her stomach like a vise and she bit her lower lip against the hard ridge of pain. For the millionth time, she questioned herself. Could she do this? If Alex found out who she really was, there was no telling how he would react.

The truth was she had no choice.

Her heels crunched through rust-colored leaves as she walked up the stairs of his home, an ornate renovated brownstone. Inhaling the earthy fragrance of the air calmed her nerves.

How she loved autumn! The season was especially beautiful in New York City. But lately, she'd been so busy trying to raise funds for Beacon House, the adult literacy center she'd founded and struggled to keep open, she barely noticed the warm days blending into cool nights.

She'd simply…existed.

She desperately needed the substantial donation she would receive if she succeeded in teaching Alex to read in three days. Failure was unthinkable, and she would do whatever it took to avoid it.

She reached the landing, sucked in another deep breath, pressed the doorbell. Chimes amplified the fresh wave of panic that rippled through her. She spotted a jack-o'-lantern perched on the stoop next door. The ghoulish sentry seemed to mock her with its crooked smile, and she stuck her tongue out at it in defiance.

Just then, the door swung open. Startled, she jerked backward and grabbed hold of the railing to avoid falling off the edge of the stair.

Good Lord.

Her heart scampered into her throat and her eyes widened at the man towering before her.

Album covers and magazine pictures did not do the brother justice. Nearly six feet tall with dark honey-caramel skin and a body that looked like it was made for a woman's most scandalous dreams, Alex was more than fine. He was "now-that-I've-seen-U-I-can-die-now" gorgeous.

A tenor saxophone dangled like an upside-down question mark from a navy blue lariat around his neck.

The large instrument looked like a child's toy nestled against his bare chest and flat, ripped abdomen.

Stop staring! She knew it was rude, yet she found she couldn't help herself.

"Miss Williams?"

Although Cara sensed Alex speaking, her attention focused on a serpent tattoo curled like a vise around the taut muscles of his upper right biceps. The head and forked tongue licked his bent elbow, igniting her curiosity, and she wondered if he had more tattoos and if so, where they were located on his body.

Face flushed, she lifted her eyes to discover he was staring right back. A frown tugged at the corners of his full lips and his fingers gripped the edge of the door, as if to warn her he could slam it shut at any moment.

His voice, a rich baritone that could melt ice, finally reached into her ears, pulled her back to reality. But when she opened her mouth to answer him, nothing came out.

Before she could try again, he shook his head and with an agitated sigh, began to close the door.

Cara leaped forward. "W-wait!" Her voice so loud it echoed in her ears.

He paused, one hand braced against the jamb, the other on the doorknob, brows lifted, waiting. Her heart stopped for a moment and she gulped back her surprise. Met his eyes and forced what she hoped was a confident smile.

"Yes. I'm Cara Williams."

She put her briefcase down, wiped her palm on the side of her skirt and decided against shaking his hand. She didn't want to risk getting the door slammed in her face.

"Sorry if I'm early. I guess I'm eager to get started, given our overall time constraints."

He was silent, choosing instead to let his eyes speak for him. They trailed down and over her body, as if exploring the twists and turns of a melody on his horn, and she fought the urge to look away under his gaze.

Alex reached for her briefcase, his fingers grazing hers, and she tried to ignore the sensations prickling a path from her knuckles to shoulder.

"Come on in," he said, but there was no welcome in his voice.

She thanked him, stepped inside, and her ears twitched as multiple locks clicked into place behind her. He strode past without a glance, leaving her confused and disappointed as he led them down a short hallway to the living room.

Cara's eyes were drawn to a magnificent grand piano that held court in one corner. It seemed to lord over the sheets of manuscript paper scattered on the polished wood floor around it.

But that was nothing compared to the Grammy Award enclosed in glass and the cluster of gold records hanging in an alcove to the right of the piano.

The visual impact of who he was and what he'd accomplished in his career made her knees wobble. She was relieved when Alex placed her briefcase next to a black leather couch and motioned her to sit down.

A bead of sweat trickled down her spine as she watched him unhook the sax from the lariat around his neck, slide the reed off the mouthpiece, wipe the instrument with a cloth and place it in the case.

His gentleness made her feel like she was observing something more intimate than mere ritual, like a father who suddenly reaches out to ruffle his child's hair as he tucks him into bed.

Without a word, he got up and walked over to the piano. Shifting in her seat, she clasped her hands together in her lap for courage she did not feel.

"You don't seem too thrilled that I'm here."

Alex's hand wavered just before he pulled the cord on the music lamp, extinguishing the glow over the black and white keys.

He turned and looked at her. She held her breath, wishing she had insisted the sessions take place at Beacon House. She felt out of her realm here, away from the familiar surroundings of her storefront office.

"You're right." His voice held a hard edge. "I'm not."

He knows. Panic sliced through her and she exhaled in dismay. The knowledge that there were thousands of people with the last name "Williams" in New York City did little to console her.

When she didn't answer, he reached for a stack of papers and started to crumple them with one hand, the sound like kindling popping in a fire. He tossed them into a metal trash can already overflowing with their discarded brethren. There was no anger in the motions, only a touch of resentment.

She found her voice, forced it steady. "I don't understand. I was hired to give you private reading lessons."

"My manager hired you." He stuffed a few survivors into a briefcase she hadn't noticed before and thumbed down the latches. "Not me."

Her secret was still safe.

Relief flooded Cara's body, but she was more confused than ever.

She swallowed the lump in her throat, removed the

contract from her purse. "There must be some mistake." She held it out. "Your signature is right here."

Alex waved away the document. "You don't need to prove it to me, Miss Williams. The fact is Tommy signed the contract in my name. That's what he does when I'm out of town or unavailable."

She peered at the signature. It *was* barely legible, and since it had arrived via fax, she'd just assumed it belonged to Alex. The mistake could cost her.

"Usually he lets me know the nature of the contract before he signs." He lowered the cover on the grand piano with ease. "This time, he did not."

She clutched the contract like a lifeline and watched him walk to the window. He stared outside and Cara could hear the sounds of children playing outside.

"I got back into town late last night. Tommy called me this morning. Dropped the bomb that you'd be coming here. Then he told me why. I called your office right away but there was no answer."

She was afraid to ask the question, but asked anyway. "Why were you trying to reach me?"

He turned, folded his arms and leveled his eyes at hers. "To tell you I have no intention of learning how to read. Not now, not ever."

Her stomach plummeted, and for a moment she couldn't breathe, couldn't think. His tone was indignant, the words decisive and not to be challenged. But he didn't know she never gave up on her students and she wasn't going to start now. Especially when she had so much at stake.

Still, contract aside, he had to want to learn how to read or else there would be little chance for success. She had to convince him to continue with the lessons, to believe he could do this.

A sudden burst of energy rocked her body. She set aside the contract and smoothed her skirt.

"I'm sorry Tommy didn't communicate with you." She kept her voice calm, chose her words more carefully. "You have every right to be upset."

Alex flopped down on the far end of the couch, leaned back and slung his arm over his eyes.

She swiveled her legs to face him. He turned his head and gave her a pointed stare.

"I can tell you this. I don't need a tutor," he retorted, his voice razor-sharp as he jabbed his thumb into his chest. "Even if I did, I should be the one doing the hiring."

Her face burned with anger. Although she knew he was simply blowing off steam, completely understandable in this unusual situation, she had to look away to maintain her composure.

Alex tapped her arm and it pulsated with heat, sending her heart rate to the moon. She turned, hoping her reaction to his touch didn't show in her eyes.

"Look, Miss Williams," he said, his voice several notches softer. Her last name got lost in a yawn. "As you can see, I'm exhausted from my trip. I'm sorry about the inconvenience, but there's no deal. I can't do this."

She unfolded her arms at her sides. "If it's my qualifications you're worried about, I can assure you th—"

"You don't get it, do you?" He leaped from the couch, his voice thundering off the walls. "I should fire Tommy for pulling this stunt, but I can't blame him. He was just trying to protect me."

Her eyes paced with him as he walked in front of the huge marble fireplace until he stopped and leaned his elbow on the mantle.

She got up and took a few tentative steps toward him. "Protect you? From what?"

"My record company! While I was in Europe, they set up a book tour of elementary schools in Harlem. But they…" His voice trailed off and something seemed to deflate within him.

"Don't know you can't read," she finished.

"Bingo."

Their eyes locked, and now that Cara was standing closer to him, she saw his were hazel, the irises speckled with bits of green. She was momentarily mesmerized by their unusual hue and the intense shame color couldn't hide.

So that's why he's so angry. Although he would probably never admit it, she could see in his eyes he was afraid. She had to tread lightly, or she'd lose him to that fear.

Alex parted his lips like he was going to say something else, but instead he stalked away.

She trailed after him. "Well, it is kind of a cool way to introduce your music to a younger audience," she offered. "I know if I was a kid, I'd be excited to see you in person."

A few feet away, he swung around and stared at her like she had two heads. "It's a waste of time! Kids are listening to hip-hop and rap, not jazz. Armstrong, Coltrane, Miles and Ellington—they've never heard of them. If it ain't sampled or doesn't have enough bass to blow their eardrums out, they're not into it."

His eyes shifted to the overflowing wastebasket, then back to her.

"When does the tour start?"

"Week from today," Alex grumbled. "Tommy's trying to get it pushed back."

Cara ran her hand through her curls before walking over to where he stood at the window. "Learning to read is very difficult for anyone, especially for adults. It's not something you want to attempt on your own."

He whirled around and pointed at her. "I told you I'm not interested. I've gotten along fine my whole life and nobody's gonna change that. I'll handle this book tour fiasco in my own way, in my own time, not anyone else's."

He turned and jabbed the windowsill with his knuckles, as if to emphasize that the matter was closed. Still, even his taut arms and the harsh finality of his words rang hollow.

Both of them knew there was no escape from what lay ahead.

He put his forehead against the windowpane. "Tommy is the only one besides my mom who knows about…that I can't…" His voice ebbed away and he shook his head. "He's been with me for years, through everything, almost since the beginning of my career."

She gazed at the muscular expanse of his bare back and a sense of protectiveness winnowed through her. She wanted to wrap her arms around his trim waist and pull him away from his fears. She had to make him believe in himself, and in her.

She approached him, placed her hand on his arm, hating herself for what she was about to say. His skin felt warm and the muscle underneath tensed as he turned to look at her. "It sounds like he really cares about you, and helps you out a lot. But what if, God forbid, something happens to Tommy. What then?"

His shoulders slumped in reply and she knew she'd hit a nerve. Then his eyes, those beautiful hazel eyes filled with pain, bore into hers.

When he finally spoke, his voice was hoarse and splintered her heart. "This can't get out. If it does, it'll destroy my career."

As a high-profile musician and one of the hottest bachelors in Harlem, she knew the media would have a field day if they learned he was illiterate.

"No one will know. I promise," she assured him, keeping her voice light in spite of the emotions churning within her. "I live a very quiet, boring life and I'd like it to stay that way."

"I don't think anything about you would qualify as boring."

She bit her lower lip with pleasure, although she was unsure whether he meant it as a compliment.

"Tommy told me about the big money I'm going to give to you."

She shook her head. "You mean *donate*. None of it is going to me personally. It's going to fund Beacon House."

He gave her a curious stare, then shrugged. "It doesn't matter because you're both nuts. There's no way I can learn how to read in one weekend," he insisted.

She nodded. "You're right. You won't be able to read *War and Peace,* but I promise you'll be able to read a simple children's book by Monday."

Alex shoved his hands into his jeans, revealing a thin line of hair at the base of his abdomen that Cara longed to trace to its final destination.

He sounded doubtful. "I guess I don't have a choice."

She looked him in the eye. "Of course you do," she asserted. "You can quit, but look at your options. If you do the tour, your record company is happy and no one knows a thing. If you don't do the tour, it'll be a PR nightmare. I'm willing to bet they already sent out the press release, right?"

"Yes. My publicist was overjoyed. At least one of us is happy."

"So, what reason could you possibly give for backing out now?"

He smoothed his hand over his perfectly round, bald head and gave a sigh of resignation. "I guess the dog ate my homework wouldn't fly, would it?"

She grinned. "It's going to be okay. I promise," she said, reassuring him. "If you don't want to continue with the reading lessons after the tour, you don't have to. But regardless, your secret will be safe."

And so will mine.

Alex stared at her a moment, and Cara knew he was debating whether to trust her or not. She had to figure out a way to make him feel at ease with her…and soon.

Slipping his hands out of his pockets, he pushed away from the window with his shoulder. "I'm going to take a quick shower and finish packing before my limo arrives."

Panic sluiced through her veins. Tommy had told her Alex's schedule was clear for the weekend. They needed to spend as much time as possible on the lessons and not be disturbed. "Limo? What limo?"

"The one taking us to my home in the Catskill Mountains."

A knot formed in the pit of her stomach. "But I thought I was going to be teaching you here, in Harlem."

He shook his head. "I'd already planned to spend a long weekend in the mountains. I'm supposed to be relaxing, remember? I'm not changing those plans for anybody. Is that a problem?"

The reality of his words hit full force and a shudder of excitement went through her.

Alone with Alex in the Catskills. Where there were no taxis, no takeout and no escape? She was already a hot mess about being with him in his Harlem town house.

She wasn't scared of him, just unused to being alone with a man she was attracted to for an extended period of time. Her dates were few and far between, and most of them never made it as far as her bed. Devoted to her work, the words *sex* and *social life* were missing from her personal dictionary.

There's really no need to worry, she told herself. Alex was her student. She was his teacher. The lines were clearly drawn. Remembering how he'd looked at her at the front door, she, like most women, knew when a man was attracted to her.

And Alex Dovington most certainly was not.

The same could not be said for her.

It was difficult not to stare at him as he stood there, maddeningly out of reach, body cut and chiseled to perfection like a Renaissance statue. The man was off the hook, and off-limits, yet her eyes yearned to do what her lips could not—devour him.

His shoulders moved forward, snapping her back to reality.

"Sorry. I lost my train of thought for a second. That'll be fine. I just need to run home and pack. I should be back in a couple of hours."

He nodded, and she kept her eyes on him as he walked out. After he left, she grabbed her purse and dug for cab fare.

He popped his head in the room and she dropped her bag in surprise. "Oh, I forgot to tell you. I was an absolute terror in school. My teachers hid behind their desks when I walked into the room. Fair warning."

His voice was stern, but she detected a hint of a smile on his lips.

She arched an eyebrow. "I guess I'll just have to get creative to keep you interested."

Where did that come from?

Judging by the odd look on his face, he was just as surprised as she was.

"If you want to grab something to drink before you leave, the kitchen is at the end of the hallway. Help yourself."

Cara waited until he went upstairs, and then drifted over to the little alcove where gold records ornamented the wall. Tucking a curl behind her ear, she gazed at the Grammy Award, but her thoughts were elsewhere.

Had she been flirting with him just now?

She almost laughed out loud. *Absolutely not.* When it came to devising enticing lines to attract the opposite sex, she got a big, fat F.

Passing the piano, her feet kicked something out of the way. Looking down, she saw a balled-up piece of manuscript paper that had somehow escaped burial. She glanced over her shoulder before picking it up.

Smoothing out the wrinkles with the palm of her hand, she hummed the melody. It was the tune he was playing when arrived. Smiling, she refolded the music and stuck it into her purse.

On her way to the kitchen, her smile faded when it suddenly struck her that there were no pictures of Alex's friends or family around, not even of his brother, Michael.

Every small room in her own apartment was filled with pictures, memories frozen in time. She cherished each one, especially the ones of her mother who died when she was nine years old.

Shouldering her purse and briefcase, Cara selected a bottle of juice from the fridge. Her mind wandered to Alex's numerous records, the U.S. and European concert tours, the sold-out performances at jazz clubs across the country and the world. All were trophies to his artistic talent.

But where were the tributes to his personal life?

As she closed the front door, the last thing she heard was the faint sound of water spraying in the shower, re-igniting her nerves. Soon the biggest challenge of her life would begin. She sank down on the stoop, leaned her head against the cold iron railing, and prayed.

Chapter 2

Alex shoved his cell phone into his duffel bag, leaned his head against the window and wished he'd never come back to New York. The gray waters of the Hudson River were dappled in the sunlight as his limo traveled north to the Catskills.

The nasal-knife voice of his publicist still rang in his ears. Word had gotten out about the tour. She was going nuts fielding calls from around the tristate area and as far away as Chicago and Los Angeles. Everyone wanted Alex Dovington to read and perform at their school. Local and national media wanted exclusive coverage and personal interviews.

What a joke.

He eased back into the leather seat and reached for the familiar green bottle. Tipping it back, he enjoyed a long swig. If they knew he couldn't read the label of his favorite beer, or damn near anything else for that matter, they wouldn't want him.

He closed his eyes and tried not to think about what would happen if people discovered his secret. He could almost see the tabloid headline:

Playboy Dummy!
Harlem's Hottest Saxophonist Is Illiterate

The familiar anger rose within him and he gritted his teeth against it. No matter how much he'd already accomplished in his career, in some people's minds, he would be branded as unintelligent. But he wasn't stupid. He just couldn't read.

True, there were some words he recognized by sight. Ones he'd picked up over the years just by living life. *Women. Sex. Money. Music. Jazz. Bar. Liquor. Nightclub. Police. Beer. ATM.* A reluctant grin tugged at his lips. Those were among the most important words in the world. At least in his world.

Everything else was a cloud of letters he could never see through. A jumble of puzzle pieces he could never hope to solve.

The cold beer felt like heaven raining down his throat as he took another long pull. He snuck a glance at Cara. If his teachers had looked like her back when he was in school, he definitely wouldn't have dropped out in the ninth grade.

She sat diagonally from him, reading a newspaper, one slim leg crossed over the other. Her hair billowed out from her head and cascaded down her back in tiny spirals of brown curls spun with gold. He wondered if it felt as silky as it looked.

She lowered the paper for a moment to turn the page and Alex got another glimpse of her face, although the caramel-colored beauty of it had captured his mind the moment he opened his door and found her standing there.

His eyes roamed down the cream blouse and over the navy skirt, all buttoned-up and properly pressed. They curved down her legs, all the way to the peek-a-boo pump dangling from her left foot as it kicked out a sporadic rhythm. No stockings, he noted with pleasure.

Bare legs, one shoe half off, and the wildness of her hair stirred a crazy kind of longing within him. *Hmm,* he thought. Maybe she wasn't all business, all the time.

An image popped into his mind. He pictured her lying beneath him, those gold-brown curls moving like waves over the pillows, her fingers linked with his as he plunged into her. Again and again. Gazing into those soft, almond-shaped brown eyes until they slid shut from pleasure and then—

Her shoe dropped with a soft thud on the carpeted floor. Averting his gaze, he turned his head toward the window and jammed a fist under his chin. He closed his eyes, willed his erection to relax.

Now wasn't the time to be hot for teacher.

He *had* to finish his new tune this weekend. On Tuesday morning he was due in the studio to record his ninth, and hopefully not his last, album for Sharp Five Records.

The muscles in his abdomen tightened with dread. Mo "Money Man" Lowenstein, President and COO, was breathing down his neck. Sales of his last two albums were lower than expected and Mo had threatened to release him from the label.

And now he had to worry about learning the ABC's? His eyes snapped open and he nearly let out a cynical laugh.

Sharp Five Records, one of the largest, most well-respected labels in the music business, specialized in jazz, R&B and world music. Being cut from the artist roster would be a major blow to his career, and there were plenty of cats lined up ready to take his place at a moment's notice.

He lifted the bottle and grimaced as the now-warm remnants of his beer hit his throat. Although Alex dreamed of starting his own label and developing his own pool of talented musicians, he knew it was an impossible goal.

How many business owners couldn't read? He gathered the answer was zero, unless they were as good at hiding it as he was.

He sighed and looked out the window at the blur of trees going by. Life was so much simpler when he was playing for change in the 125th Street subway station. He wondered if he'd known back then that the music business was more about business, and less about music, would he be sitting here today?

He thought about the manuscript paper strewn all over his living room floor. It seemed like he'd rewritten the tune a thousand times, but there was still something missing. He'd hit a wall, and whenever he tried to fix it, it sucked even worse than before.

Could the problem be writer's block? He hoped not. If it were, that would scare him more than losing his recording contract. He knew if he lost the ability to compose music, he just might give up playing forever, because it was the only part of his life where he had complete control.

And if he couldn't play saxophone and compose, what would he do with his life?

He checked his watch and blew out a breath. They'd been on the road for just over an hour, but it felt like an eternity. And they still had about an hour before they reached Cottage Valley Falls, the town where his home was located.

When they'd gotten into the limo, he'd offered Cara a beer, but she'd refused and chose mineral water instead. And that was the last time they had spoken.

The reason why suddenly hit him like a ton of bricks.

Cara was the first woman, the only woman, who knew he couldn't read, and it made him feel like he had been caught by his mother with his hands down his pants.

She knew he couldn't read a menu in a restaurant, the warnings on a bottle of medicine, his royalty statements or countless other things. And that was way too much knowledge for him to be completely comfortable around her.

He frowned and tried not to squirm in his seat, feeling exposed and trapped at the same time. Still he had to find some way to get through this weekend and get back to what was important: making music.

One of the advantages to being a bachelor was he didn't have to justify anything to anyone. The other good things about being single escaped him for the moment and he chalked it up to jet lag, not the fact just being in Cara's presence made him want to forget about a lot of things.

Alex studied her, half wishing she'd put the paper down. What was so interesting she had nothing to say to him? It was almost as if she didn't want to be there, either. Although she'd played down the donation part and seemed excited about teaching him, it could have all been an act.

From the little he'd observed about her so far, she was somewhat aloof but radiated a quiet confidence.

She seemed less like a gold digger and more like the type who wrote letters to the editor or maybe even the President of the United States.

Chicka-bow, chicka-bow, chicka-bow-wow. The Commodores "Brick House" broke through the silence in all its polyphonic glory, courtesy of his cell phone.

Kiki. He swore under his breath and saw Cara jerk the newspaper forward, but she still didn't lower it.

Since he couldn't read the address book, Tommy had programmed a different ringtone for every person in his phone. The man had quite a knack for choosing just the right tone for the individual.

Steeling himself for an argument, he retrieved the phone from his bag and flipped it open.

The first few seconds of the conversation were pleasant, until he broke their date for that evening. When there was a break in Kiki's angry tirade, he gave her his standard line and hung up.

Leaning his head against the seat, Alex exhaled in relief. Out of the corner of his eye, he saw Cara lower the paper, her full lips turned up in a smile.

"What?" he scowled.

"I'll call you, baby," she said in a mock gruff voice, then burst out giggling. "I guess she's pretty upset, huh? I think the tourists in Times Square could hear her yelling."

Alex shrugged. "She'll get over it." *They all do,* he thought as he watched Cara refold the newspaper. When she finished, it looked like she'd never opened it.

"I hadn't heard of her. Kiki, wasn't it? She must be new in your scene."

His forehead crinkled in mild annoyance, although her curiosity pleased him at the same time.

"What do you do, follow my social life?"

She gave a little laugh, stowed the paper in her briefcase, then cocked her head toward him.

"It's not difficult. You're in the press a lot." She curved the index and middle fingers of both hands for emphasis. "The Bad Boy of Jazz, always dating the latest 'it' girl."

It wasn't his fault he was popular with the ladies, but for reasons he didn't understand, he wished Cara wasn't aware of the celebrity gossip that dogged him like a vulture. He shouldn't care what she thought about him, but he did.

"So I like to have a good time," he snapped. "So what?"

She held up a hand. "I'm not hating on your lifestyle. I was just trying to get you to smile. Or at least talk to me. You haven't said a word since we got in here."

Alex arched a brow, surprised and inwardly happy she'd noticed. "You were busy reading, so I figured, you know, that we'd each do our own thing."

Her smile in response lit up the inside of the limo, and his heart. The knot in his stomach loosened a bit, and left him confused and tongue-tied. This woman was riding hard on his emotions and didn't even know it.

His eyes drifted down to the briefcase by her feet, and he managed to clear his throat. "What paper are you reading?"

She hesitated a moment and it was all he could do to keep from tearing his eyes away from her warm gaze.

"The Harlem Gazette."

Alex noted her slender arms as she reached for her water bottle. Her wrists were small and he imagined a pearl bracelet would look nice encircled around them. But other than small silver hoops in her ears, she wore no jewelry.

"It's an independent newspaper that's been around for over fifty years and one of the first black-owned newspapers in the country," she added. "I also read the *New York Times* and the *New York Post*."

His heart sank, for he knew those papers all too well. The reviews of his music hadn't been so glowing lately, but the tabloids were more than willing to publish his picture with a woman hanging off his arm claiming him as her "man."

None of those women understood that he wasn't interested in a serious relationship. He was married to his music and his career. No one got in the way. Until now.

He gripped his beer tighter. "I recognized the word *Harlem* but that's about it."

She clapped her hands together. "Good!" Her face lit up like a thousand stars and she leaned toward him. "What other words do you know?"

He opened his mouth to run down the short list, but for some reason didn't want to risk offending her. She seemed so straitlaced, but not in a nerdy way. On the contrary, the conservative getup was appealing. He wondered if it was real or just for show.

That hair. Those legs. All wrapped up in a very pretty package he didn't dare touch.

He hedged an innocent smile. "Not too many. A little bit of this, a little bit of that."

"I see. That's perfectly normal. It's not uncommon for adult non-readers to be able to recognize some words."

"Adult non-reader? Is that what I'm called now?"

"It's a little awkward-sounding, I know," she acknowledged with a wan smile.

"It's better than some of the things I've been called."

With a grimace, he faced her and memories flowed into words.

"You know, I used to ride the subway to school and I'd see men and women in suits reading the newspaper. They all looked so smart and so important."

He swallowed hard, looked past her at the countryside rolling by. Suddenly aware of what he was about to say, he hoped she would stop him from making a fool of himself. But Cara remained silent, patient, waiting for him to continue.

He met her eyes. "Sometimes I'd sneak a peek at what they were reading, and even though the words always looked jumbled up, I couldn't keep my eyes away. Those letters were like a drug."

A band of dread, mixed with anger, tightened around his chest as he thought about all the times in his life when he tried to make sense of a word, or a group of words, and failed miserably.

"One morning, I was standing next to this man reading the sports section and I couldn't stand it anymore. Before I knew what I was doing, I pointed to the caption underneath the picture and asked him what it said."

Alex felt his spine go rigid and he downed the rest of his beer before continuing.

"He gave me a funny look and said real loud, 'That's the guy from the Yanks who struck out last night and lost the game, bottom of the ninth, you can't read that?'"

Shame hooked its claws and dug into him like it had happened yesterday, and he bowed his head and traced his finger along the top of the beer bottle.

Her voice snuck past the pain. "How old were you?"

"Fourteen," he replied. "A short time later I stopped going to school."

It was the only time he'd ever given up on something.

When she didn't say anything, a knot of embarrassment sank low into his stomach. Avoiding her eyes, he curved his hand around the back of his neck and leaned his elbow against the door.

He felt stupid for confiding in her, a perfect stranger. Yet it was her eyes, caring and warm, that drew him in and caused him to talk about a story he'd never shared with anyone.

Why her? Why now?

He felt a tap on his knee, turned and found Cara sitting right beside him, so close he could smell her perfume, a faint scent of vanilla tinged with rose.

"I want to show you something. May I?"

Before he could respond, she took the empty beer bottle and placed it in a cup holder.

She grabbed his right hand, squeezed it gently. The simple gesture startled him into immediate attention.

"There are twenty-six letters in the alphabet."

He tried to break contact with her before she noticed that his palms were beginning to sweat, but she held firm.

"I know," he said, distracted because he really liked the feel of her hand on his. "Even I watched *Sesame Street.* What's your point?"

At that moment, she tightened her grasp and leaned in close to him, as if she was about to reveal a dark secret.

"Be patient, I'm getting to it."

Drawing back, she turned his hand to reveal his palm. He looked down, relieved to see it didn't look as moist as it felt.

"To start to learn how to read, all you have to remember is that there are five vowels." Slowly she traced each vowel on his palm with her fingertips.

"A-E-I-O-U."

He hitched in a breath as each letter became an invisible imprint, fingernail upon flesh, leaving a trail of indescribable sensations radiating from his palm to his fingertips.

"The rest of the letters are called consonants." She circled her finger in the dip of his palm. "Consonants and vowels work together to form words."

Alex held his breath as she tugged each fingertip down to his palm until his hand was enclosed inside both of hers, warm and gentle.

"The ability to sound each one out individually, then as a whole, is the basis for learning how to read."

Their eyes met and he thought he saw a flicker of desire in hers. But when she dropped his hand right away, he dismissed the notion. Cara had a lust for letters, not him.

"That's it?" his voice doubtful.

"Yes, that's it!"

He pressed a button on the console in front of him and spoke to his driver. "Hey, Frank! Turn this beast around. It's back to Harlem, my man, we're done back here."

Cara giggled. "No! That's not what I meant. Of course there's a lot more to it than that. But at its roots, language is made up of consonants and vowels, kind of like the basic building blocks of music are notes and rhythm."

Leaning forward, he pressed the button again. "False alarm, keep going."

He settled back in the seat, eyed her skeptically. "How do you know so much about music? Are you a musician?"

"No." A shy smile crept across her lips. "Well, maybe. But, I'm just an amateur."

He formed a square with his fingers and looked through them like a camera, appraising her. "Hmm… let me guess. You're a singer."

When she blushed and nodded, he swore. "I knew this was a bad idea."

He reached for the intercom, but Cara swatted his hand away.

"Do you have a problem with singers?"

He crossed his arms. "Yeah. Too much drama."

She drew an imaginary halo around her head and batted her lashes like a movie star. "Me? Drama?"

Enchanted, his lips curved. It seemed there might be a playful little devil ready to bust out of all that innocence.

"So you *can* smile," she teased. "Was that so bad?"

His smile faded, although it struck him funny how a word or two from Cara could turn his mood from happy to sad and everything in between. He moved away and watched the river flow, as wide and vast as the emptiness in his heart.

Sure he had a great career, plenty of money and had dated some of the most desirable women in the world.

But at what cost?

So far, nothing he'd achieved had erased the guilt he lived with every day. Deep down, he feared learning to read would only make it worse.

An hour later, Cara woke with a start to discover she'd fallen asleep on Alex's shoulder. She sat up, her face burning with embarrassment. The driver swerved to avoid a pothole and she yelped in surprise when she crashed back into Alex's side.

"I guess I should get the driveway paved." He grabbed hold of the seat. "But I'm not up here too often and I always forget how bad it is until I come back."

Cara gripped the armrest and righted herself. "I just hope we make it there without cracking our skulls open."

"Don't worry." His thumb jerked up to the ceiling. "It's padded."

Her lips twisted. "But my head isn't."

The limo bucked and Alex caught her in his arms. "Whoops!"

They laughed uncontrollably as the vehicle continued its wild ride up to his house.

By the time they arrived, her stomach hurt. It had been such a long time since she laughed so hard, she'd forgotten how good it felt.

Alex cleared his throat. "We're home."

Her heart did a slow somersault as he held her, the heat from his body enveloping her own. Although his embrace was accidental, it felt purposeful, as if she belonged in his arms.

Her chin tilted up and she saw eyes sparked with interest that went beyond a hearty laugh. He ran a finger down her cheek, dislodging a strand of hair stuck there, stroked it briefly, let it fall against her.

She broke away, trembling, and slid to other side of the limo. Warning bells went off in her head, and she had no one but herself to blame.

What had she been thinking, tracing letters on his palm and fingertips in a way that would have made Big Bird blush?

Excitement darted up her spine remembering the

feel of his hand in hers. His palm, slightly rough around the edges but soft in the middle, the fingertips callused from years of playing the saxophone.

She'd never done anything like that before. But the grace of her touch hadn't lasted long. Almost as quickly as he opened up, he shut her out again. Yet just then he didn't seem to mind having her in his arms.

What was happening between them?

The driver opened up the door and she stepped out, wide-eyed. With its rough-hewn logs, wraparound porch and gabled roof, the quaint little cottage was the perfect mountain hideaway. She fell in love with it at first sight, but her heart raced again at being in such close quarters with Alex.

The air was cooler here than in Harlem. Smelled better, too. Rubbing her arms, her nose twitched as she inhaled the heady evergreen scent of giant fir trees that surrounded the cottage. Somewhere nearby a stream gurgled, completing the Zenlike setting.

Alex appeared at her side, instrument case in hand. "What do you think?"

"It's beautiful."

His hazel eyes brightened. "Thanks. C'mon. I'll show you around."

He guided her by the elbow as they walked. Her heels teetered over the pebbled walkway. Her heart raced anew at his touch.

Was it her imagination or did his hand linger before he released her elbow to unlock and open the front door?

He showed her the gourmet kitchen, the powder room and the laundry room. With an inner frown, she realized there were no pictures of family or friends here, either. Although everything was model-home neat with modern furniture and artwork, it still felt empty. Did Alex feel it, too?

He picked up their bags and they ascended the stairway to the second floor. "This is the guest room." He set her belongings down and pointed down the hallway. "My bedroom is down there and the bathroom is in the middle. There's a linen closet halfway with plenty of towels and soap. I'll leave you to unpack."

Cara nodded and stepped inside the tiny room. Jets of sunlight poured through curtained windows. Besides a dresser and a small nightstand, the bed took up the most space.

It's big enough for two.

Closing her eyes, she indulged in an intimate fantasy of her and Alex on it, doing everything but sleeping.

"Are you okay? You look like you're going to fall asleep standing up."

She whirled around, her left breast grazing his bare arm, and nodded.

"I—I guess I'm still a little tired from the drive."

Stepping back, she crossed her arms, trying to ignore the exquisite tingling radiating through her chest. Time stopped while his eyes scooped and swept over her body like a pleasure bandit, leaving a trail of tight nipples and heat smoldering in her belly. The room seemed to shrink into nothing but unmet need.

Alex cleared his throat. "Ready for lunch? Frank drove up yesterday and stocked the kitchen for the weekend."

"Sounds great," she replied, relieved he broke the silence. "After we eat, we must get started. There's a lot of ground we have to cover."

Alex grunted low and frowned as if to say, "Not *that* again!" and left the room, closing the door behind him.

She changed into jeans and a scoop-necked blouse, then flopped on the bed and stared at the ceiling, shaken and frustrated by the encounter.

What was his deal? He'd start to relax, but when she brought up the reason why they were here, he clammed up. She wanted to believe it was only fear. But what if it wasn't?

She didn't understand him at all, nor did she understand her physical reaction to him. And at this point, she wasn't sure which was worse.

While it was normal for her to care about her students, her feelings for Alex had begun to brew a long time ago. With him, her concern didn't start with paperwork. It started with a plea for justice.

Thirteen years had passed since her father, Crawford Williams, a powerful New York City judge known for his tough rule, had sent Alex's brother Michael to prison.

As always, tears sprang to her eyes whenever she recalled the day she learned her father was responsible for breaking up families across the city.

She had been flipping through the channels, doing her homework and eating dinner, alone as usual, when she caught the tail end of a television news story.

In it, a mother was giving a statement to a reporter on the courthouse steps. Through her tears, the woman told him that she'd written a letter to her father requesting leniency for her son.

"Did the judge even read it?" she said with a shriek that tore at Cara's heart. "I asked him at my son's sentencing. He wouldn't answer and threatened me with contempt of court. If he'd read it, he'd know Michael is innocent!"

She started weeping harder, and a sullen young man

Cara learned later on was her son Alex put his arm around her and led her down the steps.

She remembered the reporter turning to the camera, his voice grim. "There goes another casualty of Judge Williams's notorious crackdown on gangs."

She sat riveted in front of the screen as he continued. "Neighborhoods are safer, but at what price? With sons and daughters, brothers and sisters behind bars, New York families are suffering through harsh jail sentences handed down by Williams that apparently no amount of letter writing or phone calls can take away."

Cara remembered racing up the stairs to her father's office in disbelief, praying that what she heard was all a mistake.

Although aware of her father's stance against gang-related activity, she didn't dwell on it or anything having to do with his job. Whenever he was home and talked about his cases, she feigned interest just to please him. He was under the impression she wanted to be an attorney, when all she really wanted him to do was love her.

She found the letter on his desk and was horrified to see more stacked in a box, some opened, some not.

In it, Alex's mom described how she and her son were devastated by his brother Michael's incarceration. Although no details of the case were given, the purpose of the letter was clear: a desperate plea for leniency that was ultimately ignored.

The anger and pain of Alex's mother so mirrored her own feelings about her father that the next day she told him she wanted to be a teacher. By sharing her love of learning with young people, perhaps she could make a difference. Heal people's hearts, not hurt them, like her dad did so well.

He never forgave her.

Even now, the hollowness she'd felt that day hit her full force, leaving her sick to her stomach.

She wrapped her arms around her pillow and thought about the special bond she'd felt with Alex ever since. In the letter, his mom had mentioned that both Alex and Michael were musicians. For years, she had watched Alex's career blossom, listened to his music and followed his love life, while he didn't even know she existed.

A lump welled in her throat at the irony of it all. A tragedy in *his* life had prompted her to make a positive change in her own that had eventually benefited hundreds of people.

She thought of the challenges many of her students faced. Heart-wrenching, gut-twisting situations most people couldn't imagine were an everyday part of their lives. Homelessness, domestic violence, alcohol and drug abuse, joblessness, not to mention low self-esteem and feelings of inadequacy. Whatever their plight, it was often related to their illiteracy.

Her students came to Beacon House with the hope and desire to change their lives. It was her mission to help them get there. She wanted to do more, needed to do more, but without the necessary funding she was strapped.

Hot tears streamed down her face and she swiped them away, feeling helpless and overwhelmed. Lately her emotions were running higher than ever. But at least now she had a chance to make things right again.

She hugged the pillow and turned toward the window.

Teaching Alex to read was critical to the future of Beacon House, and he wasn't going to make it easy. She had to figure out some way to get past his fear and reach him.

She thought for a moment. He had a job he loved, money and worldwide acclaim. But there had to something he was unable to do. Some dream he'd never achieved because of his illiteracy. She just needed to find out what it was…and fast.

Chapter 3

Thirty minutes later, Cara was eagerly arranging her teaching materials on the coffee table when the sound of glass breaking and a loud curse sent her on a mad dash to the kitchen.

"Is everything okay?" Her heart pounded and her fingers grasped the edge of the doorway.

"Yeah, that's just the way we announce mealtimes around here," he joked and dumped a pile of blue glass into a nearby garbage can.

She giggled, relieved he wasn't hurt.

He retrieved two more glasses from a cupboard and started filling them with ice from the refrigerator.

She moved toward him. "Mmm. So tempting."

Alex looked over his shoulder at her as ice cubes spilled onto the floor. "Excuse me?" he said in a shocked voice.

She laughed and gestured to an island where a

mouth-watering tray of deli meats, assorted cheeses, dill pickles, fresh Italian bread, a tricolor pasta salad and a giant pitcher of iced tea were waiting to be eaten.

The confused look on his face was priceless, then his eyes widened in recognition. "Oh…right. The food."

She pursed her lips. "What did you think I was talking about?"

He flashed a grin, flexing his muscles like a bodybuilder preening before the judge's table. "My cover-model looks, of course!"

Unable to resist, she picked up an olive. But instead of eating it, she threw it at him.

"Hey!" he shouted when it bopped him on the shoulder.

Alex selected another olive and good-naturedly chucked it at her. "You *do not* want to get in a food fight with me," he warned.

"Oh, yeah?" she taunted, deflecting the green orb with her elbow, before picking up another and tossing it his way. "Why not?"

"Because," he said, reaching up and catching her olive with one hand before dropping it into his mouth. "You'll lose every time."

He grabbed a whole handful and like a pitcher getting ready to throw a fast ball, prepared to attack.

"Okay, okay!" she shrieked, grabbing a napkin off the table and waving it back and forth in surrender. "Truce!"

Alex pumped his fist in the air with a triumphant "yes!" Rich and melodious, the sound of his laughter was like one big hug.

After washing their hands, they loaded up their plates, both a bit cautious of the other, and sat down at the table. As Alex poured the iced tea, Cara admired a bunch of wildflowers stuck into a jelly jar.

"What's the occasion?" she asked, before she bit into her ham and swiss on rye.

"My mom always told me flowers make a table. She said even if you're drinking Kool-Aid and eating macaroni and cheese on paper plates, as we often did, flowers can make it seem like caviar and champagne."

"What types of flowers did you have?"

He looked thoughtful. "When times were good, carnations from the florist down the street. They'd always last real long." He paused, and his shoulders sagged a little. "When times were lean, there were always plenty of dandelions to choose from in Central Park."

She smiled, eager to know more about the woman she'd only met through a letter. "Your mother sounds wonderful."

"She's my rock. I just wish I'd get to see her more often. Now that I'm done touring, I should be able to spend a little more time with her." He bit into his sandwich piled high with roast beef.

"Does she live in Harlem, too?"

Alex swallowed and shook his head. "Not anymore. I bought her a place in Brooklyn a few months back."

Cara felt a pinprick of fear. "Oh? Whereabouts?" she asked, somehow managing to keep her voice steady.

"Park Slope."

Phew, she thought, glad to hear his mother didn't live in Williamsburg, the Brooklyn neighborhood where she lived that was just east of Park Slope. Although it was unlikely she'd ever run into her or Alex, she didn't want to take any chances.

He took one of the wildflowers out of the jar, inhaled its scent, a faint smile upon his lips. "I would have bought her a place near me," he continued, "but she wanted to get out of Harlem. Go somewhere different. I guess memories can do that to a person."

He replaced the flower, and the smile disappeared, eyes clouded over. "Ever since my…" He stopped and took a bite of his sandwich.

"Your what?" she blurted.

The look on his face could have melted concrete. Tension stretched between them and made itself at home.

Way to go, Williams.

When it came to Alex, her natural curiosity went into overdrive. Yet she knew from past experience that sometimes being nosy about someone else's life could lead to more questions about her own. And in this case, that would be a disaster.

Alex looked stricken as he sat there, toying with his pasta salad.

"I'm sorry. It's really none of my business."

She saw something dark flicker in his eyes and vanish.

He waved her apology away, swallowed deep. "My twin brother, Michael. He…left," he swallowed deep. "And my mom hasn't been the same since."

Twins. A lump rose in her throat.

She'd heard that twins shared a strong emotional connection with their other half, even inside the womb, and wondered if Alex and Michael had that type of relationship. They must have.

Then why weren't there any pictures of Michael anywhere?

"I'm sorry," she blurted again. And she was sorry for him, more than he would ever understand.

He pinched the bridge of his nose and then suddenly got up. Cara winced as his chair scraped the floor.

"Would you excuse me?" he said without looking at her.

She bit her lip, remained silent as his plate clattered in the sink and he stalked out, the screen door slamming behind him.

Elbows on the table, she pushed her plate aside and threaded her fingers through her hair, not caring now if she messed it up.

She felt bad about bringing up the past, but unconsciously a part of her wanted to hear Alex talk about her father and what he'd done to his family. She hated keeping secrets, and it could have been an opportunity to tell the truth. Clear the air. Maybe the fact that she was Judge Williams's daughter wouldn't matter to him.

But she was lying to herself, because she knew that it would.

Thirteen years had gone by. Long enough to forget. It was also long enough to remember.

Michael had to be out of jail by now. Unless the crime was so horrible he was still locked up.

She shuddered at the thought, glad Alex wasn't involved. She was a huge fan of his music and respected him as an artist.

She couldn't allow her feelings to go deeper than that. Like any other woman, she knew that falling in love with a musician had extreme heartbreak already built into the package.

Especially someone like Alex, who was all wrapped up in a tight, muscled body that just about knocked her into the next century simply by looking at him.

She had to forget about his past…and his body. The

most important thing was getting the lessons started and they weren't getting anywhere by avoiding each other.

She had to find him.

She washed the dishes and then stepped outside, hoping he wasn't far. The afternoon sun, although filtered by the canopy of leaves overhead, warmed her face.

Moments later, she peered around the edge of the house and spotted Alex on the deck. He was stretched out on a lounge chair, eyes closed, right arm shielding his face. His shirt was off and wedged behind his neck.

She started to walk around the corner, stopped short. Although she never thought herself a voyeur, this was an opportunity she couldn't pass up.

Her eyes traced the hair on his muscular chest all the way down to where it disappeared beneath the waistband of his jeans. A quiver of pleasure swelled deep within her loins and feathered up into her abdomen. She wondered how he could look so sexy doing absolutely nothing.

Normally, she didn't get turned on just by looking at a guy, but Alex was no ordinary man. She'd fantasized about him for years; the sound of his voice, the color of his eyes, the feel of his skin.

Everything.

She leaned against the side of the house, closed her eyes and tried to clear her mind of any thoughts that could get her into trouble.

Alex was within arm's reach, yet still untouchable. It was scary and frustrating at the same time, because even if she had the courage to act on her desires, she couldn't cross the line. It would be very unprofessional. Not only that, she might lose control, and that was something she never did.

To her, losing control meant she needed him. Her

stomach did a little flip. What would she do if she couldn't get enough?

Opening her eyes, she clenched her fists against the warmth pooling low in her belly. *No màs.* The brief contact she'd initiated in the mini-lesson would have to be enough to satisfy her longing.

Just as she was going to announce her presence, her nose did it for her.

"God bless you," he called, after her loud and obnoxious sneeze.

"Thank you," she said in a pinched voice, coming around the corner. "I was just coming to find you." She stood a few feet away from him, covered her mouth and sneezed again.

His eyes opened. "So I heard."

Her heart skittered and for a second she was afraid he knew she'd been watching him. But unless he could see through walls, that was impossible. Until her allergies gave her away, she'd been out of his line of sight the entire time.

She dragged over a lawn chair and sat down. "Ready to—" her body bent over at the waist and she sneezed a third time "—get to work?"

Alex covered his ears. "Good lord, woman. You sound like a foghorn in reverse."

"I do not!" she retorted and sneezed again, hating the sound.

"It's this place." She waved her arms around above her head. "The fresh mountain air. I think I'm allergic to it. You're a New Yorker. You know what I'm talking about."

He laughed. "You got that right. It's why I bought this place. To escape from a lot of things, the air included."

She tapped her fingers on the armrest and wondered what he was trying to escape from. "Are you okay?"

His eyes met hers, crinkled at the edges. "I'm good. It's just been a long time since I talked about my family with anyone."

Relief that he wasn't mad flowed through her. "I'm glad to hear that. I'm far too nosy for my own good."

"You're a teacher. What do you expect?"

She put her hands on her hips and glared at him. "What do you mean by that?"

He sat up and swung his legs over the side. "Chill out. All I meant was the best teachers like to ask questions. They don't accept the status quo. They're always trying to learn new things."

She raised her eyebrows. "It sounds like you hold the profession in high regard."

Her breath hitched in her throat as he pulled the lounger closer to her chair. Her eyes delighted at the hair on his chest, small tight curls, just the way she liked it.

His voiced dropped low. "I'll put it to you this way. I've never met a teacher I haven't been able to, eventually, drive crazy."

The grin on his face would have made a devil proud. Her skin tingled in bewilderment. She wasn't sure if he was flirting with her or just kidding around.

As always, the man was an enigma.

She cleared her throat. "I see. Well, what you don't know about me—I mean, us—is that we can sense when a student is stalling."

She wanted to laugh at his wide-eyed, innocent stare, but held it in as he put a hand over his heart.

"You can't mean me?"

"Yes." She poked him in the chest. "You."

"Ow, woman. There's a law against carrying concealed weapons, you know."

Alex started to lie down again, but Cara stood up, grabbed him by the hand and pulled him to a sitting position. No easy feat.

"Oh, no, you don't. Come on, big boy. Time for school."

He groaned in mock protest as he slid open the patio door and stepped aside, allowing her to go in first.

Cara took her place on the sofa, while Alex sat on the easy chair. She patted the spot next to her.

"Sit here, please," she said, rummaging around in her briefcase for a pencil.

"You don't have a ruler in there, do you?"

Two can play at this game.

"Maybe, maybe not," she bantered.

He moved next to her, pointed at the magnetic letters in front of them and made a face. "You're not planning on teaching me how to read with those, are you?"

"Why not? They're very effective tools for learning."

"Yeah, right." He sniffed, crossing his arms. "Maybe for someone still in diapers."

She sighed in exasperation. "Will you just trust me? I know what I'm doing here."

He linked his hands behind his head, leaned against the pillows and stretched out his legs, lips curved in a sullen yet sexy smile.

"Okay, okay. You're the boss."

She pursed her lips slightly and tried not to stare at the triangular patch of hair at the base of each muscled arm. His nipples budded hard from the cool air. All of that combined with the faint scent of his cologne was slowly driving her crazy.

Oh, my.

"Can you please put your shirt on?"

His smile deepened. "Why?"

"Because I can't teach you when you're half-naked, that's why. Just put it on. Please."

He rolled his eyes and she ignored the urge to give him a playful swat on the behind. He went outside and snatched his shirt from the chaise longue. She had to admit she enjoyed watching his muscled abdomen contort as he pulled it over his head, and she was sorry to see it disappear under his shirt.

He sat down. "Thank you. Now what I'd like you to do is put each one of these in alphabetical order."

Alex cracked his knuckles. "Piece of cake."

He arranged the letters from *A* to *Z,* humming "The Alphabet Song" as he went along. He ended the tune in fake falsetto, holding the last note like an opera diva.

Although she was glad he knew his letters, playtime was over. She had a literacy center to keep open and he had a reputation to maintain. It was as if he'd forgotten the reason they were doing this in the first place.

"Are you always like this?"

"I warned you." He laughed. "I haven't even pulled out my best material yet."

She fought to keep impatience out of her voice. "Let's try to stay focused, okay?"

"I'm sorry." He folded his hands in his lap like a choirboy. "You have my complete attention."

"Next, I'd like you to point to each letter, say it aloud and see if you can think of a word that begins with that sound. I'll write the word on the whiteboard as you say it. I'll go first."

"*C.* Cup." She printed the word neatly. "C-U-P." She put her finger under each letter. "*Cup* begins with the 'kuh' sound." She put the next letter on the board. "Your turn."

Alex glanced at the board, then at her. "This all seems so elementary. Are you sure we just can't—"

"English is a sound-based language," she interrupted. "You'll learn faster if you can hear the sounds at the same time you read them."

She pointed at the letter. "Just take your time."

His brow furrowed in concentration as he looked at the board.

"It looks like the letter *B*."

"That's right, and what sound does the letter *B* make?"

He moved his lips, and she felt bad as he struggled to figure out the sound. But she had to test him a little, to see how much he knew.

He blew out a harsh breath. "I'm sorry. I can't do this."

She put her hand on his knee. "It's okay," she said soothingly. "The sound of the letter *B* is 'buh.'"

"B-Buh." He repeated the sound after her, then several more times. "Beautiful." He turned to face her.

His eyes held hers, and her cheeks flared hot.

"Wh-what?"

"You asked me for a word that started with the sound 'buh,' and I'm giving you one. Beautiful."

She stared into his eyes, dumbstruck for a moment, wondering why he would pick that particular word, knowing he couldn't be referring to her, hating herself for wishing that he was.

Alex waved his hand near her face. "Earth to Cara." She jumped and the dry-erase pen rolled onto the floor. "And I thought I was supposed to be the one falling asleep in class."

She ignored his comment and brought out another letter.

"*F.* Hmm..." He rubbed his fingers under his chin as if pondering a theory.

"Keep it clean!" she warned, her insides fluttering.

"I was going to say *Fudge.*" An innocent smile played on his lips. "What did you think I was going to say?"

"Never mind," she murmured, her face warm. "Great job."

"Do I get a gold star?"

She grabbed her magnetic letters. "Perhaps, but there's a lot more to do."

"Wait a minute." He took the letters from her hands and set them on the table.

She looked up at him, a little stunned by the heat that flowed from his fingers as he placed her hand in his.

He paused, like he was trying to find the right words. "I want to apologize for giving you a hard time back in Harlem."

His eyes searched hers, and the sensual feel of his thumb as he rubbed it back and forth over the ridge of her knuckles made it difficult for her to concentrate. She was sure he could hear her heart pounding.

"It's okay," she stammered. "It must have been difficult coming back and finding all that stuff out."

He nodded, not taking his eyes off hers, sucking her in and surprising her with the desire she saw there, making her want to drown in it.

"It was, but I had no right to take it out on you and I want to apologize."

She watched his full lips as he spoke to her, and when her mouth began to water she slipped her hand from his.

"You already have. The thing you have to do is to

keep at this. I know it's hard, but I'll help you. No matter how long it takes.

"And—" she winked "—if you promise to stay on task, I promise…" She quickly racked her mind for ideas and blurted out the first one that popped into her head. "I'll make dinner tonight!"

He leaned back against the pillows with a grin that could light up a city block. "Now that's one offer I can't refuse."

Two hours later, Alex braced his palms against the tile and gritted his teeth as cold water streamed over his body. Arching his back, he shivered more from disbelief than discomfort even though he felt like he was going to explode.

He never would have guessed learning the ABC's would be such an incredible turn-on.

He didn't know what it was about Cara, but he was so attracted to her he could barely concentrate on what he was supposed to be doing. Instead, all he could think about was making love to her.

For him, the afternoon had been a lesson in restraint.

He had to stop himself from tugging on the bun in her hair to release her unruly curls, from caressing her neck and stroking the outside of her thighs when they brushed against his. Her full lips had his complete attention when she spoke, even if the subject matter didn't.

He smiled and wondered whether if he kissed her her caramel skin would glow like it did when he teased her. How would it respond if he were to taste her?

Thinking of her in his arms, he didn't need to look down to know his erection was still at the ready, with no means of release other than by his own hand, and he knew doing that would be wholly unsatisfying. It would just make him want her even more.

His teeth chattered as he sucked in his breath and wished he could make the water colder, even though it was like ice right now.

Alex grabbed the soap and thought about how much he enjoyed flirting with her. Still, it unnerved him that his initial fear of talking to her was starting to disappear. He didn't like the fact he let down his guard a little too easily around her, often without realizing it until it was too late.

First, he'd told her the story of the man who humiliated him on the subway. She didn't have too much of a reaction to that one, or at least one that he noticed. Being an adult literacy teacher, she'd probably heard all sorts of horror stories.

But when he talked about his brother, told her Michael was a twin, he noticed right away the look of shock that came over her face, like she'd seen a ghost or heard some devastating news.

Although he found it odd she would react that way, he supposed many people would be surprised if they knew he had a brother, let alone a twin. He didn't discuss Michael, or any part of his private life, with anybody.

The women he dated were only interested in his money and VIP status, and the press was so busy trying to keep up with his bachelor escapades that they rarely bothered to dig into his past.

That was a good thing.

Pain filled his heart and he squeezed his eyes shut to try to make it go away. But it never did.

His mind reverted back to Cara. If she ever discovered what he'd done in his past, she'd have a different impression of him than she did right now, he realized with a frown.

She probably already thought he was a nut, and he had nobody to blame but himself for his behavior. Happy and joking one minute, storming off the next. But he'd been that way for months, maybe even years. He'd been in a funk so long he'd lost count. It wasn't exactly depression…he just didn't give a damn anymore.

Alex sighed as he twisted his body around to rinse off. So many times during his life he'd been unable to connect with a woman in a personal way.

He spent his days and nights performing, rehearsing, teaching, touring and countless other things that he had to do in order to be able to call himself a professional musician. His hectic schedule didn't leave a whole lot of time for himself or anyone else for that matter.

He stepped out of the shower and toweled off. While he balked at being in a serious relationship with any woman, in the back of his mind, he knew he was missing out.

He stood naked in front of the full-length mirror. In his mind, he saw Cara, her hair spiraling over her shoulders, wearing nothing but desire. The lush curve of her ass, soft breasts tilted up, back arching, hands reaching, and she belonged only to him.

His eyes slid shut, but the image remained and teased.

Go away!

Music was all that mattered in his life. He'd made a conscious choice to be alone, and nothing was going to change that.

Almost against his will, Alex moved closer to the image of Cara in his mind. A few seconds later, his eyes jolted open when he made contact with the mirror. Face contorted in a grimace, he looked down and hoped he'd be able to train his body, and his mind, to stay away from her.

Meanwhile, Cara was downstairs frantically searching for a cookbook. After offering to make dinner, the turnaround in Alex's attention span was downright miraculous. Now she was kicking herself for her kindness.

She knew her way around a take-out menu and could order a meal in several languages. But the kitchen? Foreign territory she didn't dare tread unless there was a powerful yet easy-to-use microwave and a stack of frozen meals in the fridge.

After opening every cupboard, pawing through all the drawers and coming up empty, she blew out a breath and anchored her hands around her hips. She was on her own.

She opened the door of the king-size stainless-steel refrigerator, her eyes widening in amazement. All this food for one man?

Then she remembered Alex was supposed to be entertaining Kiki tonight. Maybe the woman ate as much as he did. *"Chick-a-bow, chick-a-bow, chick-a-bow-wow,"* she mumbled under her breath.

Checking the meat drawer, she found a couple of strip steaks. An avid fan of cooking shows but normally too busy to try any of the recipes herself, she knew she could broil the meat quickly.

After turning the oven on, she found some red potatoes, a package of frozen green beans and a large head of lettuce. She filled two pots with water and set them on the stovetop to boil, made a tossed salad and concocted a simple marinade for the steaks out of olive oil, garlic powder and ground peppercorns.

All without having a nervous breakdown.

She breathed a sigh of relief, then frowned when she realized the only thing missing was some bread, one of her favorite foods and an absolute must-have part of her diet.

She moved toward the pantry and spotted a large, unopened box of biscuit mix.

After a quick glance at the instructions, she opened the package and removed the plastic bag from inside the box. She tried to pull it apart, but used too much force and the bag suddenly exploded, spewing biscuit mix everywhere.

She started to clean up the mess, but stopped when she heard the water going off upstairs. Alex would be down any minute and she wanted to get the biscuits in the oven before he got there.

After pouring what was left of the mix into a bowl, she added milk and frantically began to stir. Just as the dough began to form, she heard the rhythmic hiss and splash of water. She lifted her head and yelped as both pots boiled over.

Spoon clattering to the floor, she sprinted to the stove and turned the gas down under each burner. Whirling around, she leaned against the counter and was fanning herself in relief when Alex walked into the room.

He stopped in his tracks and his eyes grew large.

"Let it snow, let it snow, let it snow!" he hummed. The amused expression on his face made her cheeks tingle.

Flustered, she picked up the spoon and tossed it into the sink. "So I had a little trouble making the biscuits."

She swiped a few loose strands of hair off her face. "And I forgot to put the potatoes on to boil, the steaks on to broil, and well…" Her voice trailed off. "The truth is…I don't know how to cook."

His eyes twinkled. "Well, then, let me help you."

She started to protest, but Alex was already pitching in. He put the steaks in the broiler and added the potatoes and the green beans to their respective pots while she began to roll out the dough.

"Hold up. You're doing it all wrong."

She turned her head to look at him and her breath caught in her throat. He was standing so close that she could see a tiny nick on the edge of his jaw where he had cut himself shaving.

"And I suppose you know the right way?" she countered.

He nodded, a mysterious gleam in his eyes that made Cara's stomach do a one-eighty. "There's a special, yet mostly unknown technique to making biscuits. Now it's time for *you* to get schooled." He winked and gently nudged her aside.

"First you need to prepare your surface, so the dough won't stick." His voice held a tone of grave solemnity and Cara masked a smile as he scattered flour on the counter and spread it with his palm.

He rubbed a little flour on the shaft of the rolling pin and a thousand thoughts went through her mind, none of which had anything to do with making biscuits.

Her pulse quickened as Alex guided her right hand up to grasp the handle of the rolling pin and went into a full gallop when he reached around her waist to do the same with her other hand.

Cara craned her head toward his, eyes full of questions. His only answer was a smile as he laid his hands over hers and laced their fingers together, his hip hovering against her waist.

"Now apply firm, but gentle pressure," instructed Alex, his cheek next to hers, his voice lower than usual.

His warm breath caressed her ear, curled her toes. "Like this."

His chest, wide and hard-muscled, pressed into her shoulder blades, and she inhaled the fresh scent of soap and spicy aftershave. Heat from his hands and fingers penetrated hers and she grasped the handles tighter to keep her hands from slipping.

Together they eased the rolling pin over the dough, his body close enough to tantalize but far enough away to tease. Back and forth. Forward and back. Every so often, her breasts would skim the counter's surface, nipples budding instantly. Lips parted in a trancelike thrill.

Both bending and rolling. Both feeling and desiring.

Eyes half-lidded, her buttocks swished against the silky fabric of his basketball shorts, discovered the hard length beneath. The brief contact left her wet and tight and hungry with need.

Alex abruptly stepped back, their damp fingers stuck together briefly as he loosened his grip.

"Looks like you've got the hang of it now."

She opened her eyes and turned to face him, tingling with desire, already missing the presence of his body near hers.

She inhaled deeply. "What's the next step?" she said eagerly.

He handed her a glass. "You can cut them out with this."

Twenty awkward minutes later, they sat down to eat. When they both reached for a biscuit at the same time, they laughed and the tension was broken.

"Like minds, like biscuits, I guess!" laughed Cara.

He laughed, then gave her a strange look.

Her smile faded. "What's wrong?"

He reached across the table and dabbed her cheek with his napkin. "There's a little bit of biscuit mix here," he murmured, his touch gentle. "There. All better."

She touched her hair and wondered if it too was flecked with biscuit mix. She must look like a mess. "Thanks."

While Alex poured the wine, Cara took the first bite. "Mmm!" she exclaimed.

"I propose a toast." He lifted his glass. "To teachable moments. I think we both learned something today."

She was stunned, and more than a little scared, by the flash of heat that rocketed through her body as their eyes met in silent agreement.

Throughout the delicious meal, Alex entertained her with funny stories about his European tour. But while she was laughing, the headlines detailing his relationships with other women scrolled like tickertape in her head. As Harlem's most eligible bachelor, he'd dated pop stars, reality stars, Broadway stars and even a star forward in the WNBA.

A painful lump rose in her throat, urging her to face the facts. She knew that even if Alex had been flirting with her earlier, and she still didn't want to allow herself to believe that he was, it was only a tool in his repertoire of seduction.

To her, it meant everything. To him, it meant absolutely nothing.

Chapter 4

Alex slowed to a jog, lifting his shirt to wipe the perspiration from his brow. He'd woken at dawn and run ten miles through the dense forest and winding country roads surrounding his property, but it was no use.

He couldn't get Cara out of his mind.

Half walking, half limping along the path, he knew he'd pushed himself too hard. While he was in good shape, his hectic tour schedule had left him little time to hit the hotel gyms. When he reached the garden, he sank down onto the worn wooden bench.

Yawning, he rubbed his eyes and stared ahead in awe. The sun was just beginning to crest over the mountains, tinting the sky in pale hues of pink and orange, inviting the residents in the valley below to rise and shine. It was a scene that demanded to be shared with someone special.

Cara.

Her almond-shaped eyes had pierced his own as they ate dinner last night, seeming to beckon him.

No way, not happening. He'd never shown this place to any woman, and he wasn't going to start now.

With a low grunt, he stretched his sore legs and inhaled the fragrant air. Linking his hands behind his neck, he looked around, and the empty feeling he had inside ebbed away. This was his mecca, a private space he'd created in a small clearing at the edge of the forest, far away from the grit and glamour of New York City.

From the tin-roofed old shed that slanted sideways like a drunk trying to keep his balance, to the trees, the beautiful wildflowers and shade-loving plants. Here he could relax, reflect and rejuvenate. Here he could hide from the pressures of the world, and sometimes (though he didn't want to admit it) from himself.

"Soul Man" burst through the calm. Alex flipped open his phone.

"Hey, if you're planning on stabbing me in the back, could you at least do it while I'm *in* the country?" he growled.

"You're still pissed," said Tommy, his voice raspy from a two-pack-a-day smoking habit he refused to quit.

"Damn straight." Alex stood up, ignoring the pain. "You had no right to—"

"To what? Did you really think I was going to stand by and let you trash your career over pride?" Tommy's voice edged up over the sounds of clanging silverware. Alex knew he was at his favorite diner, eating steak and eggs with a side of oatmeal, and his stomach growled.

"It's not about pride, it's about principle. I'll learn to read when I want to, not because somebody tells me I have to."

"Looks like three months in Europe didn't soften you up one bit. You're still as hardheaded as ever."

Alex could almost see the old man shaking his head from side to side, something he did whenever they didn't agree on something. The gesture was almost fatherly. The fact was, Tommy was the closest thing to a dad Alex had ever known.

He ran his hand down his face, exasperated. Twigs snapped and broke on the forest floor as he paced back and forth. "C'mon, man. You know I wouldn't have signed off on something like this."

"Look, I'm sorry, but we've been over this already. You don't have a choice."

Alex scowled. "I thought you were trying to push back the dates or even cancel this stupid book tour. I don't understand why you—"

"Calm down, Alex." Tommy took a breath. "I talked to Mo late yesterday."

"And?" He stopped pacing, his stomach coiling into a knot.

"No deal."

Frustrated, he bunched up his shirt in his fist. "What did Mo say exactly?"

"He wanted to know why you wanted to cancel the book tour and I told him you were exhausted. That you needed time to recover."

"Man, that's the lamest excuse I've ever heard." Alex snorted, releasing his shirt and wiping his hands on his shorts. "You make me sound like a prima donna or something. No wonder he didn't take you up on it."

"What else could I tell him? The truth? I did my best."

"I know, I know. But can't you—"

"Listen, the bottom line is, you can't afford to make Mo mad right now."

Alex hated to admit it, but Tommy was right. As usual. He sucked in a slow breath.

"Sorry I was so rough on you. I just hate this."

"I know, man. But it'll all be over soon. In the meantime, I'll see if I can think of something else to put you back in Mo's win column."

Tommy didn't sound very convinced, and Alex knew he was just trying to make him feel better.

"By the way, how's everything going with Miss Williams?"

"Great!" Besides the fact that just looking at her lips, her legs and everything in between made him harder than he'd ever thought was possible.

"Good. And what else?" Tommy prodded.

"And," he hedged, "I'm earning gold stars and smiley-face stickers left and right. Happy now?"

"I'm talking about the tune," said Tommy dryly. "The one you were supposed to have done a month ago?"

He toed the ground with his sneaker. "It's coming along." For once, he was glad Tommy wasn't there, so he wouldn't have to lie to his face.

"I hope so, because Mo asked me about the album again. He wants it done Alex—and soon. We can't put this off any longer."

"I know, I know. Tuesday morning, Parkside Studios, 30th and Lex, 10 a.m. sharp. I'll be there," he grumbled.

"Listen, you can do this, man. Just stay focused. I've got another call coming in. Talk to you later."

Alex slapped the phone shut, slumped against a tree and gazed up at the leaves canopied overhead.

Focus. It sounded so easy, but he didn't even know what that word meant anymore.

He knew Tommy was only doing his job by lighting a fire under his butt. He had to finish the tune. *Today.* Forget learning to read. He'd deal with that, and Cara, later.

Right now, he needed to take a shower, grab his horn and get back to the shed. Checking his watch, he headed back toward the house. It was still early. Hopefully, Cara was still in bed and he could sneak back to the garden before she woke up and filled every minute of his time with her tutoring sessions.

If he was lucky, it would only take a few more hours to work out the kinks in his tune and write out the arrangement for the band.

His creativity was more active in the mornings anyway or, his lips curving into a smile, after a couple of rounds of mind-blowing sex. It had been a while, but up until this weekend, he'd been too busy to care.

Although he was trying to disguise his attraction to her, Cara was making it extremely difficult. She triggered long-dormant fantasies within him that were begging to be explored. He felt he was on the brink of unearthing something about himself he never wanted to admit.

His need for a woman in his life.

Her enthusiasm for teaching impressed him. He wished he could bottle it up and drink it down to cure the apathy he was feeling toward his own profession.

Music had been in his life for so long. And now? He didn't care about it or anything else anymore, and he couldn't figure out why.

He just knew he had to do something to get himself, and his mind, back on track where it belonged before it was too late and his career was over.

When he got home, his eyes shifted up to the second floor. The curtains were drawn on both windows of Cara's room.

He exhaled in relief. So far, so good.

He nudged the front door open as slow as he could, frowning when the rusty hinges whined anyway. He took off his shoes and socks and padded barefoot to the laundry room, where he stripped down and threw his running clothes into the washer.

He crept upstairs, wrapping a towel around his waist, praying she wasn't awake yet. But before he even got to the "amen," an unusual sound stopped him dead in his tracks.

Feet sinking into the plush carpet, he pressed his ear to the bathroom door. As he listened to the sounds on the other side, his brow furrowed with anger.

Moments later, his mind churned in disbelief as he took a step back from the door.

Cara *singing*.

The sound of the water masked the lyrics, but Alex recognized the melody immediately.

Hell, he'd written it.

The back of his neck pricked with anger. He felt like he'd been punched, and yet was disturbed by an incredible need to listen to her.

Cara's voice was beautiful. A bluesy alto, meditative and haunting, that wound around his ears and left him wanting more. The melody sprang from her so easily, while he'd been struggling with it for weeks.

But where had she found his music?

His mind snapped to attention, remembering the wastebasket overflowing with discarded manuscript. Cara must have taken a copy of his tune out of the trash. But why?

He wanted to burst through the door and confront her

right then, but hesitated, still mesmerized by her sultry voice that went straight to his gut. His body felt like it was being pulled right into her soul, but his mind was an emotional sandstorm trying to figure out how to handle the situation. He sensed he was hearing something more than raw talent. Much like the woman herself, Cara's voice was a gift yet to be discovered.

Still, she had no right to take his tune and set lyrics to it without his permission.

Regret filled his heart as he realized just how much he was beginning to trust her. He really thought she was different, that perhaps she saw him as more than the means to an end. The heat that burned between them as they rolled out the biscuits, the concern he saw in her eyes, her commitment to teaching him.

And now this?

This didn't feel like caring. It felt like betrayal. His heart rocked in his chest. Everything she'd said and done up until this point must have been an act.

What other secrets could she be hiding?

He tightened the towel around his waist. "Only one way to find out," he muttered.

Arms crossed, he stepped back, leaned against the wall and waited for the door to open.

Cara stepped out of the shower, so jittery with excitement that her towel kept slipping from her fingers as she wrapped it around her body.

Humming merrily, she opened the bathroom door and cried out in shock at the sight of Alex standing there.

His face was like stone, chasing away her happy mood. He too was clad only in a towel. It hung dangerously low around his torso, in stark contrast to the bank of rippled muscles above.

She tore her eyes away from his waist and forced a smile.

"Good morning! I was just on my way to—"

"Steal something else of mine?"

She flinched at his angry tone but managed to square her eyes with his.

"You know, I may not be able to read," he continued, his voice like ice. "But my hearing is fine."

"What are you talking about?"

He took a step forward and she let go of the door-knob.

"I heard you. Singing in the shower. Trouble is, no one but me is supposed to know that tune."

Oh, Lord. Had she been singing that loudly?

Her eyes slid shut as panic swelled. She hated having anyone hear her sing. But worse than that, after last night, she knew she had to put some distance between them. But not like this.

He glared at her. "Why did you do it?"

She knew the answer, but she wasn't ready to admit it, to him or to herself.

She opened her eyes and cringed, feeling exposed and angry, more at herself than him.

She tightened the towel around her breasts. "Excuse me, I need to get dressed."

She tried to walk past him, but he grabbed her arm.

"Not so fast. You're not going anywhere until you tell me why you took my song."

"I didn't take it! I found it on the floor of your living room, okay? You were upstairs getting ready to leave and I just picked it up. Now let me go."

She wrested away from his grasp and looked up. His eyes were blazing like fire.

"You found it?" he said, his tone scornful. "That's a crock. You stole it."

"I—I'm sorry, Alex. I really didn't think anything of it." Cara knew she was telling the truth. Because at the time, she hadn't thought at all.

"You had no right. Why didn't you just pick it up and throw it away in the trash can? You had to open it? You had to keep it? Why?"

Cara opened her mouth to speak, but no words would come out. Alex was right.

"I don't know."

He folded his arms over his chest, as if he didn't believe her. "So you just decided to steal it?"

She clenched her fists. "Stop saying that! I didn't steal it."

"What do you call taking somebody's private property?"

She stepped toward him, shivering from the coldness in his voice. "I can't explain why I did it. All I can say is I'm sor—"

He cut her off with a wave of his hands. "What do you plan to do with it?"

"Nothing, of course! I just liked the melody and then the words just seemed to flow. It's a great tune, Alex."

His lips pursed, emphasizing the doubtful look on his face.

Just then, her towel loosened and she grabbed it just before her nudity was exposed. She looked up and her face got hot, as his eyes raked over her body. Alex might have been angry, but it didn't stop him from checking her out.

"Can we talk about this later? I'm freezing and I want to get dressed."

Without waiting for his answer, she turned and started walking to her bedroom.

"You know, Cara, this changes everything."

A sliver of fear ran through her and she spun around.

"What do you mean?"

He walked up to her and stood so close that the tiny hairs on her arm frizzled from the energy between them.

"I can't be around someone who's going to steal from me."

She stepped back and threw up her hands. The towel loosened slightly but she didn't care. She was tired of him making her feel like a criminal.

"Alex, you're making too much of a big deal about this. What do I have to do to make you believe I'm sorry?"

"There's nothing you can do except get dressed and get packed. I'm going to call Frank right now and have him come up here and take you back home to Harlem, where you belong."

Cara's face reddened with anger. "Wait a minute," she exclaimed, turning around and following him as he strode toward his bedroom. "Today I was going to start you on the book I've chosen for you to read on your tour. I know you can do this."

"It doesn't matter anymore."

"Alex, please. I told you I'll give your music back. Then you'll have it and you won't have anything to worry about."

He turned and frowned. "How do I know you didn't or won't take something else?"

She wanted to scream in exasperation, but she

counted to five to calm herself. "Because I said I won't. Isn't that good enough?"

He shook his head. "You should have thought about that before. Look, I don't surround myself with a lot of people." His voice softened. "I was starting to trust you."

She grasped his arm. "Alex, you can trust me," she pleaded. "I promise you can."

His eyes held hers, and for a moment, she thought he believed her.

"I don't think so. Not anymore." Without another word, he stalked into his room and slammed the door.

Fear lodged like a stone in her heart, and she stood there trembling, until finally the chill in the air forced her to move.

Back in her room, she shut the door, collapsed and folded her arms around her knees.

If she didn't teach Alex how to read in three days, she wouldn't receive the money that would help her prevent Beacon House from closing its doors. The domino effect would be swift and negative, extending to the current clients, the community of Harlem and the thousands of unknown individuals whom she would never be able to help.

Taking that music was one of the dumbest things she'd ever done. And now it could cost her everything.

Chapter 5

Within ten minutes, Alex had dressed, grabbed his horn and was running toward the garden. His feet pounded on the hard ground, dodging tree roots fingering across the path. When he reached the shed, he plopped down on a wooden chair, breathing hard.

Maybe now he could finish his tune.

Or what's left of it.

His heart still pounded in anger and disbelief over what had just happened inside.

He shook his head, then picked up his sax and played a flurry of notes, not pausing to take a breath until he felt like his lungs were going to explode.

He wanted to kick himself in the head for being so stupid. For starting to fall for what he thought was strait-laced, sweet innocence. His mother always said he was a bad judge of character.

With an exasperated sigh, he started playing again.

His fingers flew up and down the saxophone, crushing notes and bending pitches along the way.

But all he could hear was Cara's voice. She had taken what was supposed to be an up-tempo bebop tune and flipped it into a ballad. Sweet, sultry, mystifying. Her voice invaded his mind, drowning out any musical ideas he might have had.

He smirked and let his saxophone drop against his chest. *Might* was the operative word. The truth was for the last few months, he'd been having trouble concentrating on composing, or anything else for that matter.

And now he was expected to learn how to read? With a so-called teacher who had pretty much stolen his music?

Yeah, man, like you never did anything wrong in your life.

He pushed the voice inside his head aside, just like he had the past. Or at least he tried to. He had a sinking fear the past was about to catch up with him, and what he was starting to feel for her was only the beginning.

He wasn't sure which was worse.

What he felt couldn't be love. It was too soon for that. Besides, he'd never truly loved a woman, so he wasn't sure he would know how it felt when it came along.

He just knew that despite what she'd done, there was something about her that he found extremely appealing. She piqued his curiosity more than any other woman had in a long time.

But none of that mattered now. She'd be gone in a few hours and he could get back to his so-called wonderful life.

He fingered the saxophone around his neck, the one that he loved so much, that had cost his family so much.

If his fans only knew the truth.

He tipped his head back and stared at the rusty tin roof. His breathing eased and he inhaled the dank smell permeating inside of the shed, even though he'd left the door wide open.

Right now, he felt as old as the shed smelled. Was it because he'd just turned thirty this summer or was it something else?

He inhaled again and his nose twitched at the scent of vanilla, as intoxicating as the woman who wore it.

"I just came to tell you that I'm not going anywhere."

Whirling around, he blasted Cara with a pointed stare. "Yes. You. Are. Frank will be here any minute to pick you up."

With a smug smile, she crossed her slender arms. "No, he won't."

He raised his eyebrows and fought the desire to pull her into his lap. "Oh, yeah? Why not?"

"Because you're not a quitter. You wouldn't have gotten this far in your career if you were."

"Listen, Cara." He got up and stood so close only his saxophone was between them. "You don't know anything about me," he retorted, starting down into her brown eyes. "And if you did, you wouldn't be here right now."

Fire met fire. "And leave this half-finished? No. Way."

He held on to the mouthpiece of his saxophone, never taking his eyes off hers. "Why is this so important to you?"

"I don't like to see anyone giving up on something, and—"

"Oh, c'mon!" he said, his tone mocking. "Do you really expect me to believe your holier-than-thou attitude? You were hired to teach me how to read, not to steal my music."

Her eyes widened with hurt, and he felt guilty for causing her pain. Maybe he was being too hard on her.

Alex took a deep breath, softened his voice. "I'm serious, Cara. I want the truth."

"I know it was stupid," she began, biting her lip. "But when I opened that crumpled-up piece of paper and hummed the melody, I knew it was something special."

She traced a finger down the bumpy surface of his saxophone and he groaned inwardly, wanting her fingers to continue traveling south.

"It sounds dumb, but you create magic every day, and I guess, just for once, I just wanted to be a part of it."

Her eyes bore into his, her need for him to understand so pure his skin tingled. It was then he knew she was telling the truth.

"Magic?" He snorted. "Nah, it's just a lot of hard work."

"True, but it also takes a whole lot of talent and dedication." She placed her hand on his arm, traced his tattoo with her finger, and when his groin quivered, he wished his saxophone wasn't playing referee between their bodies.

"I'm sorry, okay? You have to believe me."

He stared into her brown orbs and his heart dropped when he saw they were brimming with tears.

To his knowledge, he'd never made any woman cry. Remorse tumbled through him. He broke away from her gaze and ran his hand over his head.

"You're good, you know."

She took a step back. "I'm what?" she choked out.

"Good." He cleared his throat. "You have a nice voice."

Her smile was wary, and so sweet to behold. "Thanks. I never thought I could do it. You know, make up words to a song and have them sound like that. So perfect, like they were always meant to be together."

He smiled back, felt something good break within him. "That's what I love about playing jazz. I can get that feeling every day."

"Yeah. I felt like I was high," she confided. "Not that I would know anything about that, you know from a drug perspective that is. I fall out on cold medicine." She giggled.

He laughed. Her sense of humor always caught him off guard.

"It sounds like a dream life, being able to travel the world, play the music you love and get paid doing it."

He shrugged. "I hate to bust your bubble, but the music business isn't all fun and games and VIP parties. Do yourself a favor. Stay an amateur."

"Are you saying I have no talent?" she huffed.

"No, I already told you that you have a great voice, but this is a tough business. If something goes wrong, at least you have something to fall back on."

Unlike me.

He walked over to the bench and plopped down.

"Writing and performing every day, night after night, city after city. For those that really care about the music, for every note you play, you tear away little pieces of your soul until one day there's nothing left."

She sat down, her hair tickling his arm. "And are you one of those people that care?"

He didn't answer, while he wrestled with the part of him that wanted to tell her everything. But there was another part of him that still didn't trust her. Not because she stole his music. It was something else he couldn't quite put his finger on.

"Sometimes I don't think I have the right to care." He gestured toward his home and the forest beyond. "The right to all of this."

She poked him in the arm. "Hello-oo? Who has a Grammy Award sitting on a shelf in his living room? Trust me, I like a guy who's humble, but you need to give yourself a little more credit."

"And here I thought you were into hotheaded jazz musicians," he teased, giving her shoulder a gentle squeeze, loving the glow that lit up her cheeks.

"You know…" she paused, and her smile was shy this time "…I really *am* one of your biggest fans."

He folded his arms. "Oh, really?"

She glanced down at his saxophone. "I've been following your career for a while, and I admire you a lot."

The kindness in her eyes drew him into a place inside himself he wasn't sure he wanted to explore.

"It's got nothing to do with talent. I haven't got a choice. Music is in my blood, it's such a part of me that sometimes I wonder what it's like to be in the real world."

She tilted her head. "The real world?"

"Yeah, the one you and everyone else lives and works in. If I couldn't play music, I'm not sure I could survive."

She shook her head. "That will never happen."

If only she knew.

"Learning to read could open up a whole new world to me, one I'm not sure I'm ready for. I've gotten along this far not knowing how to read, how will I survive actually knowing how to do it? Does that make any sense?"

She nodded. "A lot of my clients feel that way. I realize it might be scary, but you're a long way off from that. Right now, I'm just trying to prepare you for the tour. After that, you can decide how fast or slow you want things to progress. I just need a little more time with you and then you'll never have to see me again."

At the thought of the weekend ending, he felt a twinge of sadness he didn't understand.

"Yeah," he muttered. "I guess we better get cracking, huh?"

He stood, walked over to the shed and shut the door. He'd have to find some way to work on his tune later. Tommy would be calling him for an update tomorrow and he wanted to be able to tell him it was finished.

Although Cara's rendition was beautiful, he would never use it on his album. For some reason, he wanted to keep her voice for his ears only.

She followed him. "Do you actually practice in here?"

"Yeah, when I don't have a beautiful woman trying to teach me the ABC's."

The smile on her face warmed his heart. In fact, her very presence had a calming effect on him, and as they began to walk down the path to the house, he had the strongest urge to take her hand in his and never let go.

When they got back, Cara headed straight for the living room where she had already organized her teaching materials. Her goal for today was to focus on the book he would be reading during the tour.

She glanced at her watch and her eyes widened. Time was definitely not on their side. She had less than forty-eight hours to get Alex to a point where he

would feel comfortable reading in front of an audience
full of children.

Not an easy task with a man who she'd rather be
lying in bed with laughing at Saturday-morning car-
toons. Their feet, legs and arms wound around each
other like a grapevine.

The fantasy disappeared when a vision of Beacon
House, complete with boarded-up windows, graffiti
and a padlock on the door, invaded her mind.

Panic crept into her veins at the consequences of failure. All her clients would have to go elsewhere for literacy services. And she would have to face her father,
who would only be too glad to comfort the loss of her
dream with one of his famous I-told-you-so speeches.

There was no way she was going to allow that to happen. Her stomach grumbled but she ignored it. It was
time to get back to work. She glanced around, but while
she had been daydreaming, Alex had disappeared. She
figured he was in the kitchen, getting lunch.

"Grrr," she grumbled. "That man!"

Just then she heard the floorboards squeak and she
raced into the hallway. She gasped when she caught
Alex climbing the stairs to the second floor.

"Oh, no, you don't!"

She grabbed his hand, intent on dragging him back
to the living room if she had to—all five foot one of her.

"You are *not* getting away this time."

He stopped in his tracks and her heart fluttered when
he turned and ran his thumb slowly over hers. When he
turned on his heel and walked down the stairs, a look of
chagrin on his face, she felt smug satisfaction.

Now we're getting somewhere.

But her victory was short-lived. Her breath whooshed

out of her when Alex suddenly put his arm around her waist and pulled her to him.

"Oh, yeah? Who's gonna stop me?" His eyes had a devilish gleam in them that Cara found hard to resist.

He rested his hands on the small of her back, and she could not help imagining them sliding down to cup her buttocks.

"I am." Her defenses weakened as he drew her even closer, until she had no choice but to place her arms around his neck or have them squished between them.

"Hmm…" She felt his fingers trace a path up her spine until they nestled at the base of her neck. "Care to show me how?"

"I—I," she stammered as he gently massaged her neck with the pad of his thumb.

"I have a variety of methods…um…that I employ for students who are chronic procrastinators."

He smiled innocently. "You can't be referring to me?"

She nodded, as tingles of sensation radiated throughout her spine. Her eyes slid shut as muscle tension melted into desire.

"Who else is in the room distracting me right now?" she murmured.

"I'm not trying to distract you. I'm trying to help you. You seemed so tense back in the garden."

Her eyes snapped open and she tried to step away from his grasp, but he tightened his hold. She wanted to lay her head against his chest, nuzzle the muscles beneath his shirt, feel his heart beating.

But she didn't.

Instead, she lifted her head and looked up into his hazel eyes. His face was unreadable and yet she sensed he was struggling, too.

But with what?

Her lip quivered slightly, but she steadied her voice. "You were so angry at me you told me to hit the road. So yes, I guess I was a little stressed out."

He smiled down at her then and she wanted to shake her head in disbelief. From the intimate way he was embracing her, it didn't seem like he was still angry. His arms, strong and warm, held on to her tightly, almost possessively.

And she didn't mind one bit.

Still, it was hard for her to fathom how he could be so forgiving so soon, when what she'd done was unforgivable. She had yet to hear it from his lips, and feel it with her heart.

"Haven't you ever heard the old saying that everything happens for a reason?" he inquired. "Maybe you taking my music will be the best thing that ever happened to me."

She wanted to ask him how that could be possible, but she was afraid of the answer.

"But I'm still not sure if you've really forgiven me. Have you?" she said, hating the uncertainty in her voice.

"It isn't easy," he admitted with a sigh, his hands heavy on her shoulders. "If you haven't figured it out already, I'm a pretty private person. I was starting to trust you, and that's really hard for me to do, especially with a woman."

"Why is that?"

He shrugged. "I'm not sure. Maybe because I've never been able to be myself with a woman. I like to have a good time, and that's about as far as it goes."

"Except when those good times hit the presses," she added. "*People, US Weekly, Ebony.* It seems like you're never with the same woman twice."

He scowled. "Some of what you read is true, to an extent. But most of it isn't. Being who I am and doing what I do for a living doesn't come without a price. Someone always wants something from you. And if they don't get it, they'll tell anyone they did—for the right amount of money."

She shook her head. "Fame. I think I'll play it safe and just watch the movie."

He laughed out loud. "That's smart. The truth is I don't open up to people very easily. Now whether that's due to being famous or just a part of who I am, I don't know. But despite everything," he said, bringing his hand to her face, "for some reason, I'm starting to feel very comfortable with you."

His words were like a dream, too good to be true, yet wasn't that what she'd wanted to hear all these years? A part of her desperately wanted to believe him. The other part screamed, "Watch out girl, he's a player!"

She pushed both thoughts to the curb as he traced the underline of her jaw with his finger. She closed her eyes, succumbing to the allure of the roughened tip against her soft skin, the feel of his arms around her.

How many times had Cara wished it was her in the glamorous designer gown holding his arm on the red carpet, at the latest club, or dining at the finest restaurants?

But the reality was this: he was a famous musician who made a habit of courting beautiful women, while she made a habit of cozying up with a good book. He was totally out of her league, and if she didn't wake up out of this fantasy, she would lose the only thing she cared about—Beacon House.

She stopped his hand with her own and wriggled out of his grasp.

"I think it's time we got back to business."

At her professional tone, Alex opened his mouth like he wanted to argue, then nodded his head. "Okay, but on one condition."

She cast him a wary glance. "Sure, what is it?"

"Have dinner with me tonight. It'll be fun. We'll eat, then head on over to the club."

She felt giddy and woozy at the same time. "Dinner? Club?"

"Yeah, every time I'm up this way, I sit in with the house band at the Jazz Hideaway, it's a local jazz club in town. Is that okay with you?"

She swallowed hard. "Sounds great! Now that we have all of that out of the way, can we please get to work now?"

"Sure. Let me just make us some quick sandwiches. I'm starving, aren't you?"

She nodded. Her stomach was grumbling. Plus, if they ate now, they could work until it was almost dinnertime.

"That would be wonderful. I have a surprise for you!"

"A surprise?" He raised his eyebrows. "I can't wait."

He reached out a finger and traced the roundness of her cheeks, leaving her knees shaking. "See you in class in fifteen minutes."

She blushed at the sensual undertones in his voice. As he walked down the hall to the kitchen, the heat of his fingers danced on her skin with the undeniable promise of seduction.

Chapter 6

Back in the living room, Cara's encounter with Alex left her dazed and aroused. She could no longer deny her attraction to him. Her body was telling her to go forward, but her negative balance sheet knew better. If there was ever a time to just get the job done, it was now.

But how to resist him, she thought as she sank down into the couch and flopped against the pillows.

Every time she tried to keep their interactions all business and no play, he broke through her professional demeanor with his sexy smile and a masculine vulnerability that was utterly endearing.

She'd realized a long time ago that her heart was her weakest link, and it started and ended with Alex.

He returned with lunch. "I hope you're hungry," he announced. "Turkey sandwiches on rye, pita chips and fresh lemonade."

Plate in hand, he turned to give it to her and suddenly stopped.

"What's that behind your back?"

She gave him a sly smile. "Something that will change your life!"

"Hmm." He set her plate back on the tray. "Let me guess. A baby?"

Cara laughed out loud. "No!"

Alex snapped his fingers. "Darn. Other than marriage, that's the only thing I can think of that would turn my world upside-down. Except if I won the Powerball. Now that would be cool! I'd be a gazillionaire!"

She giggled. "Well, this is kind of like hitting the lottery, at least in my opinion."

"Then what are you waiting for? Let me at it!"

He tried to reach around her waist to grab it, but Cara scooted away to the opposite end of the couch.

"Ta-da!" she shouted with flourish and held the book in the palm of her hands, directly in front of her breasts.

His eyes narrowed. "Is that the one I'm going to be reading?"

She nodded, pointed to the title. "Can you spell out the letters for me?

Her breath hitched as he moved his body closer to hers until their knees were almost touching.

He frowned. "I'll give it a try."

Putting his finger under the words, he traced and spoke each letter.

"T-H-E…"

It was impossible, but she swore she could feel the slow path of his fingertip on her skin through the hardcover of the book.

"J-U-N-G-L-E…"

At his every touch, her loins pulsated with pleasure and she shivered involuntarily. What if there were nothing between his fingers and her skin? For a moment, her imagination ran wild at the thought.

"T-R-U-M-P-E-T-E-E-R."

He stopped talking and looked at her. The fantasy dissolved and left her cheeks tingling with embarrassment.

"The Jungle Trumpeteer," she pronounced. "Very good! I'm proud of you!"

He looked skeptical. "This isn't one of these 'Dick and Jane' books is it? Because if it is, I'm not reading it. Unless—" he flashed a wicked smile "—it's the porn version, of course."

She gasped. "Be serious, okay?" she said, and pretended to smack him lightly on the head with the book. "Don't worry. This book is a simple read that will stimulate your imagination."

He grinned. "I'm going to need a lot more than a book. How are you at massages?"

Heat flared her cheeks at his flirtatious question. What had gotten into this man?

"Uh," she stammered. "That's not part of my lesson plan."

He shrugged. "Oh, well. Can't blame a guy for trying. So what's next? Should I sit on the floor crisscross applesauce?"

She burst out laughing. "One step at a time, okay? Feet on the floor and keep your hands to yourself. Do you think you can do that?"

His eyes penetrated hers and she felt his desire reflecting her own.

"I can. I'm just not sure I want to." His silken voice caressed her with unspoken meaning.

Although it was very difficult to do, she elected to ignore his comment.

"Just let me read the book to you all the way through with no interruptions."

"Okay," he said with a resigned sigh. "You read. I eat."

Satisfied that he was momentarily distracted by food, she cleared her throat and began to read.

The story was about an elephant who believed his trunk was a musical instrument. When he played it, he was able to rid the jungle of poachers and ultimately saved all the animals.

She closed the book. "How's that for a happy ending? Well, what do you think?"

No sooner had the words left her mouth than Cara had a strong feeling his upbeat mood had suddenly soured. He sat there quietly and finished his sandwich, his brow knit together as if he were in deep thought. If she had held her breath in suspense, she would have turned blue.

Finally, he leaned back against the pillows. "Thank you for not torturing me with *See Spot Run.*" He turned his head toward hers, and her heart did a little flip. "But I still don't know about all this."

"What do you mean?" she asked, sensing his trepidation.

"Do you really think I can do it?"

"Of course I do, Alex," she said softly, patting his arm, the muscle underneath tight with tension. "You have the basic concepts down. Now it's just a matter of applying what you've already learned. It shouldn't be too hard."

He palmed his head, his voice ragged. "What if I mess everything up? Those kids will see me struggling with the words and—"

"And they'll see someone who's trying to do his best," she replied firmly.

He sat up quickly and she dropped her hand to her side.

"But what kind of man doesn't know how to read?" he said in a disgusted tone. "I'm thirty years old! It's too late."

His negative words didn't surprise her. It was normal for people to feel scared and anxious about learning to do anything they thought they should have learned when they were younger. Whether it was learning to read, playing a musical instrument, riding a bike, or in her case, learning to love and trust someone.

"I have clients ranging from age eighteen all the way up to eighty. It's *never* too late."

When he said nothing in response, she reached out and touched his hand to reassure him.

"Alex, why do you doubt yourself all of a sudden?"

Dropping his elbows on his knees, he shook his head sadly. "You'll never understand."

Her heart squeezed at his comment. "Can I give you some advice?"

"Do I have a choice?"

She shook her head and smiled. "You should focus on all the things you'll be able to read once you become a better reader, rather than the things you're struggling with now."

"Like what for example?"

"What about fan mail?" she suggested. "You do get fan mail, don't you?"

"Of course, I get fan mail, both email and the old-fashioned way."

"Wouldn't you like to be able to actually read them and respond?"

"I have a publicist. That's her job."
Strike one. Think, Cara, think!
"What about love letters?" she blurted.
His eyebrow shot up. Clearly, she was grasping at straws.
"Uh, okay, but I think you're missing one thing. You have to be in love with someone to write or receive a love letter."
Cara's heart pounded. "True. Haven't you ever been in love?"
"You mean a melt-into-your-shoes kind of love?"
She nodded.
"Nope. Is that bad?"
She stared at him in disbelief. "But what about all those ladies I've seen you with on TV and in magazines? Didn't you love any of them?"
He shook his head. "I knew going into those relationships, and I use that term lightly, what most of those women wanted. Eventually, my assumption proved to be correct. They never looked or bothered to see the real me. All they wanted was status and a good time. That's it."
His eyes moved over her face, a touch of curiosity in them. "What about you?"
She shrugged. "Not really. I've been focused on building my career and trying to make Beacon House an integral part of the Harlem community."
But I can easily fall in love with you. Too easily.
"I suppose, that if I was in love, it would be nice to write a love letter and read it to my woman," he conceded, looking straight into her eyes.
Her face warmed, and she glanced at her watch to hide her reaction. It was nearly three o'clock.
"Are you ready to try again?" she inquired.

He nodded and they leaned back against the soft cushions. With the book unfolded across their laps, they began to work again. Although it was still a slow process, Alex was reading the words a little easier now.

While his concentration had improved, she could barely keep her mind on the book. As she watched his full lips form each word, she wondered if his lips would caress her body with the same care.

Not wanting to lose momentum, they stayed at it for a couple of hours, only breaking once to stretch their legs and grab some coffee from the kitchen.

Finally, Alex stood up, and Cara tried not to let her eyes drift south. But she couldn't help but notice how snugly his jeans fit around his long legs. Her breath caught in her throat as she was treated to another glimpse of his muscle-wrapped abdomen as he stretched his arms over his head.

She closed her eyes briefly, and in her mind's eye she saw him standing nude before her and she was doing more than just admiring his well-toned body.

"Cara!" Her eyes opened to the sound of snapping fingers. "Looks like you're as beat as I am. Do you mind if we stop for now? We should rest a little bit before we head out to dinner."

"Not at all." She stifled a yawn. "I think that's a great idea."

They carried the plates and glasses out to the kitchen, rinsed them and put them in the dishwasher. The otherwise mundane task didn't seem so boring doing it with him.

They walked up the stairs and Cara was about to go into her room when Alex grabbed her hand.

"Wait. I have one final question."

And before she could ask what it was, he pulled her

close and drew her into a passionate kiss that went beyond mere lust.

Cara thought she was going to die from the sensation of his lips moving softly upon hers. His tongue teased and probed the core of her mouth, drawing her deeper into him until she felt like she would collapse under the supreme weight of her longing for him.

Crushed against his body, heat was mutually exchanged, stoking an intense need that only increased when she felt the evidence of his desire throbbing against her belly.

Suddenly, he lifted his lips from hers and tilted her chin up with his fingers. She opened her eyes to meet his hazel ones, rimmed with undeniable passion.

"Is that the type of kiss you give to a woman when you are falling in love?"

Rendered speechless, she could only nod her head.

"Just checking." He caressed her lower lip, reddened from his kisses, with the edge of his thumb. "See you downstairs in ninety minutes."

He graced her with a seductive smile and she stood in amazement as he turned and walked down the hallway.

Cara slid into her room, shut the door and leaned against it.

What was that all about?

For the moment, she didn't care. She just wanted to savor the kiss that still sparkled on her lips and not think about the possibility that he might be falling in love with her.

Or that she might be falling in love with him. Both scenarios would be more than she could hope for, and more than she could handle right now.

And although she realized that his offer of dinner

was likely not meant to be a date, his kisses told a different story.

Why not indulge in the fantasy for once?

She decided that for one night, she would pretend that she was Alex Dovington's woman, his confidante, his lover. The only one he desired, needed and loved.

Dreams-come-true always seemed to pass her by. But she had a strong feeling that tonight was the beginning of a whole new adventure.

Back in his own room, Alex stretched out on the bed and closed his eyes, reliving the tenderness of Cara's tawny-pink lips, full and luscious, upon his own. It was a kiss he never wanted to forget.

But what had gotten into him, swooping her off her feet with a kiss that she wasn't likely to forget, either? Although he could play any ballad like his heart had been broken a thousand times, he wasn't the romantic type. He'd even dropped the L word!

He knew the answer. Cara.

This woman, with the wild corkscrew hair and sweet disposition, was making him do things he'd never done before. Feel things he'd never felt before.

He'd never felt so moved by desire for one woman as he was for Cara.

His erection strained against his pants, begging for some kind of release. But he kept his hands at his sides and remained still, content to allow himself to be a prisoner of his passion for her.

His beyond-beautiful, unbelievably sexy reading teacher.

Although she held a certain innocence that was appealing, he was playing with fire and he knew it.

The fact that she stole his music, with no regard to his

feelings or the consequences of her actions, was enough evidence to justify some doubt about her character. He was trying to get past it, and although her reason for doing it seemed plausible, forgiving her was difficult.

He desperately wanted to believe that she wasn't like all the other women he'd come into contact with in his life. Money-hungry, power-seeking, back-stabbing ladies who thought playing with his heart was just part of the "game."

What they didn't know is that love was never a game to him. It was a gift.

Their audacious confidence was all for nothing. Those women never stood a chance.

Cara, on the other hand, was a woman he wanted to know intimately, feel deeply, and make her his own.

She was on the opposite side of his usual spectrum of dating choices. And despite his best efforts to remain cool and detached, she was wriggling her way into his heart.

That was a feat in itself.

Ever since he'd lost his twin brother, his heart had been closed to anyone and everyone. Sure, it had happened years ago, but he could remember it as if it was yesterday. Some hurts never heal, especially when you're the cause.

Slowly, she was breaking through his self-imposed wall of bitterness and hesitation. Her patience with him for the past two days was worthy of sainthood, in his opinion. He knew he could be a real pain in the butt when he felt like it.

He remembered that when he got the news from Tommy that he'd hired Cara to teach him to read, he was angry beyond belief.

But right now, he had the strangest urge to call his aging manager and thank him.

He chuckled low. If it wasn't for Tommy, he wouldn't have experienced one of the most freeing moments in his life. One he definitely wanted to experience again.

The next time he kissed her, he wouldn't be able to stop. By the way she responded to him, he didn't think she would mind at all. She might accept him into her bed, but would she let him into her heart?

He had to admit that Cara was out of his league. She was intelligent and well-read, with an aura of quiet confidence that was evidenced in her demeanor. He loved the way she walked, dressed and spoke. She made him laugh with a sharp sense of humor that always kept him on his toes.

Yes, Cara Williams was class, elegance and playful sexiness all wrapped up in a body that would drive a blind man to distraction.

So what if she couldn't cook?

The most appealing thing about her was how much she cared about him. He could tell that about her almost instantly.

Back at his town house, when he confessed his fear of public humiliation, she acknowledged his concerns with grace. Somehow she knew how important it was to him to maintain his dignity through this ordeal.

And just now, when he was struggling to make sense of the letters and sounds, he'd felt her silently cheering him on. Her smiles of encouragement meant more to him than she would ever know.

Normally, he couldn't be forced into anything and yet here he was, kicking and screaming his way to a world he'd never known. Deep down, he realized that Cara was the key to his success.

But she could also be his downfall.

He ran his hand over his head, suddenly remembering he'd yet to put the final touches on his tune.

He'd never let any woman get in the way of his music, but that was exactly what had happened today—and yesterday for that matter. And he was horrified that a part of him didn't give a damn.

To hell with Mo and Sharp Five Records, he thought for the hundredth time.

His dream to open up his own recording and publishing company was always in the back of his mind. He wanted to be his own boss, chart his own course. Taking orders from someone had never suited him. It angered him that his very future in music hinged on the bottom-line revenue of his next album.

Instead of feeling blessed by his success, he felt trapped.

His goals had felt out of his reach until he'd met Cara, who had inspired a glimmer of hope within him.

It was too soon to tell how well he would read at the book tour, but he was starting to feel more comfortable. His heart swelled with pride, and he was surprised that he was even starting to *like* reading—a little. Words didn't seem like the enemy anymore.

His mood sobered when he remembered that she was only on contract for the weekend. When Monday rolled around and they were back in Harlem, he would never see her again. Although he sensed she was attracted to him, she'd already indicated that her first love was her work. They had that much in common.

He rose and sat on the edge of the bed to prepare for his shower. He slowly removed his pants and boxers, groaning when the hardened length of his penis sprang forth.

Better make this an ice-cold shower.

If not, he knew he wouldn't be able to make it through dinner without stripping her naked and taking her on his own wild ride.

The fantasy alone was tempting enough to make it happen right now, although he feared making love to her one time wouldn't be enough.

He knew without a doubt that he wanted and needed more than just a casual, platonic relationship with Cara. There was so much he didn't know about her that he wanted to discover.

But he cared about her enough to realize that friendship was the only fair and realistic option. She deserved the stability of a husband, not the unpredictable lifestyle of a professional musician.

Had he set her up for a fall by asking her to dinner?

No, he rationalized. She would not take his invite that way. For the past two days, she had tried to maintain a professional relationship. He was the one who had taken it to the next level with a kiss that surpassed even his wildest expectations.

Besides, if she knew what he'd done in the past, she would probably hate him. Or at least lose all respect for him. His heart grieved a little at all the mistakes he had made years ago that were still costing him dearly today.

He sincerely hoped that someday he would have the courage to tell her his story, and more important, upon learning the truth that she would have the courage to stay with him—if only as a friend.

It was all he could hope to be to her.

He heard the water go on in the bathroom, and he swore silently. Cara had beaten him to the shower— again. Knowing her, all the hot water would be gone when she was finished.

He sighed as he plopped back down on the bed to wait his turn. It looked like his wish for a cold shower was about to come true. Too bad his dream of having her in his arms forever would likely remain a fantasy.

Chapter 7

Ninety minutes later, Alex went downstairs, fully expecting Cara to keep him waiting while she did whatever women do to get ready to go out. But she was already there. And she took his breath away.

"Wow." He whistled low. "You look fantastic!"

She blushed in return, pleasing him. He took his time admiring her. His eyes raked over her gray dress with spaghetti straps that was cut low enough to tease and let him imagine the rest.

"Turn around, please."

She gave him a curious look, but then twirled slowly.

He loved the way the knee-length dress shimmered around her bare legs as she turned. It fit her well-toned body beautifully. Her curly mane was down and flowed around her shoulders. High-heeled silver sandals completed the ensemble.

She looked like an angel.

Remembering his vow to use tonight to further cultivate a "friends-only" relationship, he said a silent prayer. He could look, but not touch. Tonight, he would definitely need divine intervention to keep his hands off of her.

He smiled. "Ready to go?"

"Yes. Can't wait!"

When they reached his black Porsche Boxster, he opened the door and waited for her to get in and buckle her seat belt before he entered on the driver's side.

"I hope you don't mind riding in this."

She crossed her legs and he enjoyed watching the smooth and sexy motion.

"Not at all. I've always wanted to ride in a Porsche."

"Great. I keep this just for going into town. My limo will be here tomorrow evening to pick us up and take us back to Harlem."

He thought he detected a shadow cross her face, but quickly dismissed that notion. She was the one who said she was going to recommend another reading teacher to him once they got back to Harlem.

Clearly, she wasn't losing sleep over the fact that their weekend together was almost over.

"Do you hear that?" he said, admiring the low purr of the engine. "It's like music to a man's ears!"

She laughed. "How fast does it go?"

"As fast as you want it to go, baby!" he shot back with a wink.

She cracked up, and he laughed along with her.

"Hmm." Her lips arched into a mischievous smile. "Why don't you show me?" Her throaty voice made his palms sweat.

He grinned. "When you say it like that, your wish is my command."

After looking both ways, he gripped the steering wheel, pressed on the gas and away they went.

Cara whooped with delight as they flew around the mountainous curves at lightning-fast speeds.

It had been a long time since he made a woman so happy with such a simple, albeit somewhat dangerous, show of machismo. Normally, all he'd get was "the eye-ball roll" with a bored sigh on the side.

The evening was starting out with a bang, and he hoped it would only get better.

About twenty heart-stopping minutes later, they screeched to a halt in front of Idella's Country Carriage House, spraying gravel all the way.

"Was that fast enough for you?"

"Incredible!" she replied, her eyes dancing with excitement. "Let's do it again!"

The pure joy on her face lit him up on the inside with happiness. "There's more where that came from, but let's eat first. I'm starved."

Just then, the valet opened up the passenger door and Cara got out. Alex dropped the keys into the man's hand and escorted her through the restaurant's foyer.

"Mr. Dovington!" The pretty hostess beamed at the couple. "It's great to see you again! We have everything ready. Right this way, please."

As they walked to their table, there were curious glances from the patrons, a few waves, and a not-so-silent whistle.

Alex pulled out Cara's chair, admiring the delicate roundness of her shoulders as she sat down.

"Alex, this place is beautiful. And the view!"

The semicircular private room they were in overlooked the Hudson River.

"Breathtaking, isn't it?" He sat down and accepted the menus from the server. "Just wait till you taste the food!"

"That's if he doesn't eat it all up first!"

"Auntie Idella!" he exclaimed as he rose, smothering her with a hug.

"Stop your nonsense." Idella sounded stern, but the grin on her face was wide with happiness.

"Aw, you know I can't help giving you some sugar."

"Yeah, and it's always more than I can handle!" Idella guffawed so loudly the sound reverberated throughout the tiny room. "You know I have heart trouble! What are you trying to do? Put me in an early grave?"

He loved making Idella laugh. It brought back happy memories from his childhood, sitting in her kitchen, watching her cook and eating more than a boy should.

"Never!" His smile was as sweet as Idella's disposition. "Who else would make your famous sweet potato pie that folks drive from miles away to eat?"

She shushed him, but Alex could tell she was pleased with the compliment. "Now wipe that million-dollar smile off your face and introduce me to this pretty young lady!"

"She's the reason I've got this crazy grin, Auntie! This is Cara Williams."

"Pleased to meet you. Your restaurant is gorgeous!"

Alex handed Cara a menu. "And only the best Southern cooking you'll find outside of the South. Take a look."

Idella's face beamed. "Soul food with spunk, I like to say."

They ordered seafood muddle soup, smothered pork chops, fried corn and sweet potato biscuits.

"Excellent choices. I'll put your order in myself."

"Thank you. I can't wait!"

Idella poked Alex in the arm. "She's a keeper. Be nice to her," she warned before walking away.

"Ow!" He rubbed his arm. "I'm nice, aren't I?"

"When you want to be," Cara teased.

His eyes were only on Cara as a waiter arrived with a bottle of champagne. He poured two flutes before setting the bottle on ice and leaving.

"I think a toast is in order." Alex raised his glass to meet Cara's. "Here's to private lessons."

They both smiled as they clinked their glasses together.

His face warmed under Cara's gaze as she took a sip. "Hmm…this is delicious. If the food tastes as good as this wine, I'll be in heaven."

He gazed into her eyes. "I already am."

For the first time, he noticed how thick and natural her lashes were, and he wondered how they would feel if he ran his fingertip along them.

"In all seriousness, I'm grateful for what you've done so far. I know I can be a real bear sometimes."

Her brows raised in surprise at his confession. "I'm used to it. Most people go through a range of emotions when they are learning how to read. I just never had to sleep in the same house with them," she added shyly.

"Well, then, in that case, I am honored to have you as my guest."

The waiter set a basket of biscuits on the table. He reached for one, then stopped. "I'm sorry. I always forget my manners around Idella's sweet potato biscuits. Please, you go first."

"Thank you." Cara reached for one of the steaming biscuits, picked it up and immediately dropped it onto the linen cloth. "Ouch! They're hot!"

Alex sprang from his chair and knelt at her side.

"I should have warned you. Idella's biscuits are always pulled straight from the oven.

"Are you okay?" He reached for her hand. "Let me help you."

He blew lightly on each of her fingertips and watched as her eyes slid shut. Then he brushed his lips against each one, loving the feel of her warm fingers against his mouth.

A low ache swelled in his groin when he felt her hand tremble with his every touch. He had the strongest urge to suck on them, but instead he folded her hand in both of his and gave it a gentle squeeze.

Her eyes fluttered open, her voice unsteady. "Th-thank you. That feels much better."

He wasn't surprised when his own legs wobbled when he rose and returned to his side of the table.

"What is it with us and biscuits?"

"I remember the evening quite clearly." She gave him a knowing smile. "Ever think about trying out for *Top Chef?*"

"Not a chance. That was an exclusive lesson reserved for VIPs only."

Right now, the only woman he desired to do and share anything with in the kitchen, or anywhere else, was Cara.

Alex buttered his own biscuit. "Tell me more about yourself, Cara. Inquiring minds want to know."

"There isn't much to tell. I have a degree in elementary education and a master's in adult education from Fordham University. I have a cat named Molly. And I hate broccoli and cauliflower."

He laughed. "Me, too!" He bit into his biscuit and

swallowed, hating his need for an answer to one of the most important questions he would ask her.

"No boyfriend?"

She shook her head and his heart lifted in his chest.

Her face held a trace of sadness. "With my schedule, I don't have time for a serious relationship. I pretty much live at Beacon House."

"I know what you mean. I live in hotels and planes. It's pretty rare when I'm actually home in Harlem."

Like him, working was a means of escape, and he wondered what she was running from in her life.

"I told you about my mother, but what about your family? Do you have any brothers or sisters?"

She took a sip of champagne. "I'm an only child."

"Excuse me, sir." The waiter arrived with their soup. They both inhaled the delicate aroma that swirled between them before digging in with gusto.

He reached for his third biscuit. "What's your father like?"

Cara dropped her spoon and some of the soup splattered on the table, surprising them both.

She mopped up the drops with a napkin. "Ugh. I'm so clumsy sometimes.

"He wasn't around," she said in a smooth tone, honed from answering that difficult question countless times over the years. The people who asked were unaware that those three words were verbal knives to her broken heart.

Alex gave a sympathetic snort. "Sounds like my old man."

"I don't see him too often now."

"Why's that?"

"He and I don't agree on much of anything. So in

order to avoid getting into an argument, we tend to avoid each other."

"I see. What does he do for a living? I can sum up what my dad did in one word—nothing."

Her spoon stopped in midair. "Why all the questions about my dad?"

Her voice had a hard edge and Alex knew he'd pressed too much.

"I just thought deadbeat dads were something we had in common. So I was just curious, that's all. I'm sorry, Cara. I didn't mean to offend you."

"He wasn't a deadbeat, just difficult. I thought I knew him, but it turns out I didn't know him at all. Let's just leave it at that, okay?"

The silence between them made his heart hurt, especially when it was broken only by the low conversation and occasional bursts of laughter from the other diners.

He looked up at Cara and saw that the playful spark had gone out of her eyes. He wanted to bring it back, but all of a sudden he didn't know what to say.

It bugged him that she didn't want to confide in him. Weren't men supposed to be the ones who didn't want to talk?

If she were to ask him, he would admit that she was starting to break down his walls, but hers were evidently stronger. And he wanted to know why.

"Here we are!"

Idella swooped into the room with the rest of their food. She served them and stood back to wait for each of them to take their first bite.

Cara cut and ate a piece of pork chop, so tender it practically melted in her mouth. "Outstanding!"

Alex enthusiastically agreed. "Auntie, you've outdone yourself again!"

"You've always been a charmer, just like Michael."

Oh, God, here she goes again. He felt his body go rigid as Idella turned toward Cara.

"Honey, you should have seen them when they were younger. Like two peas in a pod, and their momma dressed them alike, too. Thicker than thieves those boys were."

Cara smiled at her. "I'd love to hear more." She hesitated and he felt her eyes meet his. "If that's okay with you, Alex?"

His jaw tightened, like it always did when somebody talked about Michael. But he knew it was futile to stop Idella. For one thing, his mother had always taught him it was rude to interrupt his elders. And even if he did ask her to be quiet, she would simply ignore him. That's just the way she was.

"I remember at one family reunion, Alex and Michael entered the potato-sack race. I think they were about ten years old."

She leaned over and nudged Cara with her elbow. "Now you'd think that because they were twins that they'd be able to work together and figure out a way to get across the finish line, right?"

She leaned back, placed her hands on her hips and shook her head. "Oh, no. They decided it was time for them to grow up and be individuals. They each had their own ideas about how to run in that sack. It was hilarious to see them, each trying to do their own thing, and none of it working."

She hooted with laughter. "Those two boys had everybody cracking up until they literally rolled over the finish line."

Alex momentarily forgot his annoyance at Idella and shook his head at the memory. "We were so mad at each other that we started fighting in the sack. Didn't even wait till we got out to throw punches."

"Your daddy had to break it up and then he tore into you," Idella recalled. "Your eyes and your tails were black and blue."

"Yeah," said Alex with a rueful smirk. "He always seemed to know when to put the drink down and show up in time to give us a whipping."

"That day, the whole family realized that the only thing Alex and Michael had in common was getting into trouble," Idella added.

"Michael always blamed me for getting us a whipping from Dad that day. He didn't speak to me for a long time. I don't think he ever forgave me."

"But I bet he's proud of you now!" Cara offered.

The jovial mood in the room deflated into an uncomfortable silence.

"Michael died thirteen years ago," Idella replied.

Cara clasped her hand over her mouth. "Oh, no!"

Alex stared at her. The stricken look on her face had him wondering why she reacted so strongly.

He wiped his mouth with a napkin. "It's nice to reminisce, but some things you don't want to remember."

Idella gave Alex's shoulder a sympathetic squeeze. "Your auntie has too much of a big mouth on this ol' body. I'm sorry, hon."

The couple was silent as she cleared away some of their dishes.

"Both of you better eat up before the rest of your food gets cold. Let me know if you want me to warm anything up," said Idella, then she waddled out of the room.

Cara started to say something, but Alex put up his

hand. As far as he was concerned, the trip down memory lane was over.

"You don't want to talk about your father? Well, I don't want to talk about my brother. End of conversation."

The candlelight flickered, seeming to mock him. The romantic evening he had hoped for had turned into a disaster.

I never should have brought her here.

He loved Idella to death. Telling old stories was how she paid tribute to people that she loved. His aunt had no way of knowing that the mere mention of his brother's name brought every emotion inside him to a screeching halt.

The truth about Michael was known only to him.

But holding the secret inside all these years was getting to be too much to bear. The guilt was eating away at his livelihood, stealing his happiness and making it nearly impossible for him to justify his own existence.

When would it all end?

Tears started to fill his eyes. He pushed his plate away so roughly that Cara jumped in her seat.

"I need some air," he announced and got up from the table. His chair almost fell over, but he caught it just in time and pushed it back in place.

As Cara started to rise, he shook his head. "Please stay and finish your meal." His voice caught in his throat at her worried eyes. "I'll meet you out front in about twenty minutes."

He left the room without another word, but not before he saw the look of hurt and confusion on Cara's face. He hated that he was responsible for putting it there. But he'd never cried in front of a woman, and he wasn't going to start now.

* * *

When Alex left, Cara felt as cold as the ice wrapped around the bottle of champagne.

Michael was dead! How? When?

She'd always assumed he was still in jail, put there by her very own father. The news chilled her to the bone and she rubbed her bare arms in a futile attempt to get warm.

It didn't make sense.

Did her father know? She doubted it. He was so concerned with maintaining his prominence in the New York City judicial system that nothing else mattered.

Not even his daughter, she reflected bitterly.

She walked over to the bay window and tried to focus on the peace and tranquility of the river below.

But it was useless.

All she could think about was Alex and the pain her father had caused his family. Her heart broke anew, especially for his mom and the desperate plea that was never answered.

She walked back to the table, her feet like lead. Pushing the plate of now-cold food aside, she was refilling her champagne when Idella walked into the room.

"Where's my hot-headed nephew?"

Cara shrugged and sipped her champagne. "He stormed out of here about five minutes ago." Her mouth quivered as she spoke. "I don't know what happened."

She turned to Idella and the kindness on her face made her eyes well up. "What did I do wrong?"

Idella patted her arm, before pulling out a chair and sitting down. The wood creaked under her weight.

"You didn't do anything, honey. That boy's been hot-headed for as long as I can remember."

Tears welled up in her eyes because she knew how

it felt to be forced to talk about something you just wanted to forget.

"This is my fault. If only I hadn't been so curious."

Idella shushed her with a wave of her hand. "No, it's mine. You'd think at my age I would know to stop talking before I put my foot in my mouth." She gave a heavy sigh. "But I can't help it. I love telling stories about my family, especially those who have passed on, to keep their memory alive. People forget about you so quickly."

Idella's voice sounded wistful, as if being forgotten hit her a little too close in the heart.

"You wouldn't know it by looking at him, but Alex has been through a lot. The death of his twin brother hit him hard, and as you can see, he's still grieving."

"How did it happen?" She didn't want to deceive Idella but she had to know.

"Michael died in jail from a heart attack soon after he was sentenced for a gang-related crime."

"Isn't it unusual for someone that young to have a heart attack?"

"Yes, his mother had an autopsy done and she found out he had a rare disorder that weakened the ability of his heart to function properly. One day, his heart just gave out and the doctors could not revive him."

Cara gaped at her. "That's awful."

Idella nodded. "When Michael died—" her voice trailed off and she dabbed at the corners of her eyes with a napkin "—Alex was never the same."

Idella's eyes scrutinized her. "You seem like a nice girl. Maybe you can bring some joy back into his life. Money and fame sure haven't done it."

"We're just friends," Cara said firmly, hoping that was still true after tonight's events.

Idella regarded her a moment, shrugged. "You can't

blame an old woman like me for hoping. Alex is very dear to me. He's my only nephew and I want to see him happy."

Cara smiled, got up and walked around the table.

She gave her a warm hug. Idella smelled like talcum powder and barbecue sauce. "He's lucky to have an auntie like you."

Glancing at her watch, she squealed. "Oops, I've got to go. Alex is probably outside in the car. I don't want to keep him waiting."

She opened her purse and dug around for a mirror. "He's taking me to a jazz club. At least, that was the plan before he left." She applied a light-colored lip gloss and powdered her face.

"Sweetie, you're so pretty, you don't even need any makeup."

Cara smiled. "Thanks. It was so nice to meet you. I wish you the best of success with your restaurant."

"Nice to meet you, too, dear. Love to have you back whenever you're in the area."

Cara started to walk out, but then hesitated.

"What's wrong?"

She turned back to Idella. "I don't know what to say to him."

Idella gave her a knowing smile. "Honey, he doesn't need your words. He needs your patience and a whole lot of love."

Cara smiled as she walked over and gave the woman another hug. "Thank you," she whispered.

"Aww." Idella hugged her. "Now get out of here and go meet that stubborn nephew of mine before I get the mind to put you both to work in my kitchen!"

Cara chuckled at the thought and waved goodbye.

When she walked out into the foyer, her breath caught in her throat.

Through the glass doors, she could see Alex outside, leaning against the back of his Porsche, talking with the valet. He was smiling as if nothing was wrong.

But she was beginning to learn the truth about the man hiding behind the façade of fame. She didn't know what would happen between them tonight, but emotionally, she felt closer to him than ever before.

She felt his eyes on her body as she exited the building. Her nipples hardened under his gaze as her mind recalled the incredible kiss they'd shared earlier.

She lifted her chin and sauntered toward him with a confidence she was only beginning to acknowledge within herself.

As she walked, her eyes took in his powerful build, clad in black designer jeans and a black dress shirt that was open at the collar. He was the most beautiful man she'd ever known.

Idella was right.

Sometimes it was the woman who needed to be strong for a man broken by the past. A ray of light through the darkness of memories. An unlikely hero.

Tonight, she would be all those things, and more.

Chapter 8

It was the longest ten minutes of Cara's life. Alex hadn't spoken since they'd left the restaurant, and the silence between them seemed even more overwhelming in the luxurious but cramped Porsche.

She wanted to follow Idella's advice, but how long would he act like she wasn't even there?

Outside it was so dark she could barely make out the trees lining the road. Cara found it hard to believe there was a jazz club out in this desolate area.

Lost in thought, she nearly jumped out of her skin when Alex slammed on the brakes. His elbow dug into her chest as he grabbed her right arm and she cried out in pain.

"Hold on!" he shouted.

The car veered sharply to the left. She screamed and grabbed on to the door handle as they rode over the grassy berm, narrowly missing landing in a ditch.

A few feet later, the car screeched to a halt and Alex slammed on the emergency brake. His hand gripped the steering wheel so tightly his knuckles looked ready to pop out of his skin.

He released her arm, leaned in close. "Are you okay?" His breathing was uneven as he searched her eyes.

Her voice shook. "I think so. What happened?"

He loosened his grip on the steering wheel. "We almost hit a couple of deer! I forgot how much they run around out here."

"City boy," she teased, rubbing her arm in the place where it still hurt from when he'd grasped her.

"Yeah," he muttered, watching her. "I don't belong here."

She shook her head, twisted away and looked out into the darkness. Not even a near-death experience could make things right between them. The silence grew, though she could feel his eyes on her back.

He hissed out a slow breath. "Listen. Are you sure you're not hurt? I know I was a little rough. It's just when I saw those deer, I panicked."

His fingers touched her shoulder. "Look at me."

She did and saw tenderness in his eyes just before he curved his hand around her neck, brought her lips to his and apologized in the sweetest way a man could.

Alex's mouth journeyed over hers, saying what he couldn't say aloud, exploring the need he found there. She captured and held on to the joy as his tongue probed deeper. Both of them reveling in the beauty of wanting, and being wanted.

He broke away, and their eyes found each other in the darkness.

"I guess nothing's broken."

Cara felt her heart soar. *He still cares about me.*

She brought her fingers to her lips. "Yes, it appears that everything is in working order."

And there's nothing like a hot kiss to break the ice, she thought, as he started the car. They pulled back onto the road without a word, yet they both knew the air between them had shifted, like it does just before dawn breaks.

She hesitated only a second before reaching over and placing her hand on his thigh, stroking lightly. His muscles twitched hard in response, and he placed his hand over hers.

She'd always heard that the best part of fighting was making up. As he rubbed his thumb slowly over the ridge of her knuckles, she trembled inside with anticipation. That kiss and this touch hinted at just how pleasurable making up with Alex could be.

A short time later, they arrived at the club. Alex grabbed his saxophone and his eyes were all over Cara as he helped her out of the car. *Now this is more like it,* she thought, warming under his appreciative gaze. Her skin tingled with excitement in anticipation of the rest of the evening.

"You're going to love this place," he whispered in her ear. "It's one of my favorite spots in the world."

He opened the door and the hot sounds of jazz poured out, beckoning them inside.

The place was small and decorated classic cool with bistro tables clad in white tablecloths scattered around the bandstand. There was a bar on her right and red leather booths on the opposite wall. Votive candles were everywhere, adding to the romantic atmosphere. Every seat was taken with people talking and laughing. She noticed more than a few women staring at her with envious eyes.

Alex led her to a reserved booth near the stage. The instruments were all set up but no one was playing, and she realized the music was coming from a sound system.

He slid into the booth next to her and pointed to the walls. "Check out the pictures!"

Cara instantly recognized Thelonious Monk, Miles Davis, Herbie Hancock, Oscar Peterson and two of her favorite singers, Ella Fitzgerald and Billie Holiday. They were some of the greatest jazz musicians that ever lived.

"Which one is your favorite?" he asked.

"I'd have to say Billie, definitely. Her voice has a rawness to it that just makes my heart ache every time I listen to her."

His eyebrow arched at her serious tone, and she blushed as she realized the same thing happened whenever she looked into his eyes, heard his voice or fantasized about being more than just his teacher.

He snapped his fingers. "You see! It's just like I said when we were riding up here from Harlem. You singers are sooo dramatic," he intoned, fanning his hand in front of his face.

She elbowed him in the ribs. "Ow!" he exclaimed, rubbing his side. "Time for a drink. What can I get you?"

"Club soda, please, with a twist of lime."

"Okay, I'll be right back."

As he walked over to the bar, a man carrying a trumpet approached her.

"Hi, you must be Candy. Ol' Alex said you were beautiful, but he didn't say you were drop-dead gorgeous!"

Candy? Who's she?

She smiled politely. "No, my name is Cara."

He laid his hand on his huge belly. "Oh, I'm sorry. I didn't mean to offend. It's just that ol' Alex brings so many beautiful babes up in here, it's hard to keep track of them all."

"No worries," she said, bristling inside. Between this and the daggers being thrown at her from the other women in the club, maybe coming here had been a mistake. She certainly didn't want to be known as one of ol' Alex's babes!

"The name is Mac, and I'm always grateful when Alex takes the time to sit in with us locals."

Cara breathed easier at the sight of Alex returning with their drinks.

"Hey, watch your back, Mac—she's mine."

The two men laughed aloud and exchanged hand slaps.

"Watch out for this man," joked Alex. "He's a monster on the horn, but a kitten with the women."

Both men cut up into a fit of raucous laughter.

"Candy knows the score." Mac guffawed and hooked his thumb toward the stage. "C'mon man, let's hit it."

When he left, she raised an eyebrow at Alex.

He flashed a sheepish grin. "Mac has always been terrible with names."

She sipped her club soda in quiet fascination as he opened up his case and slipped his saxophone around his neck. After adjusting the reed, he tapped each key silently and played a few low notes.

Moments later, the music stopped and the chatter ebbed away as Mac stepped up to the microphone.

"Good evening. Welcome to the Jazz Hideaway. Tonight we have a very special guest with us. Just back in town after a very successful European tour, put your hands together for Sharp Five Records tenor saxophonist Alex Dovington!"

He pecked her on the forehead. "Promise you'll wait for me?" Without waiting for her answer, he strode toward the stage.

"Only forever," she whispered to herself.

Loud hoots of applause resounded throughout the room as Alex counted off the beat.

"Ah-one, ah-two, ah-one-two-three-four."

The band immediately swung into a bebop groove. The bass walked the rhythm of the beat, bolstered by the steady tap of the snare and the hi-hat cymbals. All worked together to support the tune's rapid staccato melody.

Cara sat in rapt attention, watching Alex play so fast that his fingers moved in a blur up and down the keys. Stretching and bending notes at will, he made the saxophone growl, purr and bark.

His improvisation had people in the audience bobbing their heads, as chorus after chorus soared into their ears and their hearts. When he ended on a sinfully low note, they burst into wild applause.

He nodded his head in appreciation, and when he looked over at her, she gave him two thumbs up and the biggest smile she could muster.

When the rest of the quartet was done improvising, Alex picked up the horn again and played the melody out.

"Let's give a big hand to Alex Dovington!" bellowed Mac.

The band played a few more tunes before breaking to rest before the next set.

Her heart skipped a beat when Alex leaned into the

microphone and thanked the band. His baritone voice sounded even sexier reverberating through the small room.

Cara watched in amusement as a small crowd immediately gathered around the stage. Many were women, both young and old, with cameras in their hand, primping and waiting for the perfect photo opportunity. Over the next few minutes, Alex posed for every picture and signed every autograph.

If this is what it's like to be famous, she'd pass. She was glad the only notoriety she'd ever have was the full-page ad in the yellow pages for Beacon House.

Cara straightened as Alex slid into the booth next to her.

"Why didn't you warn me about the groupies? I am seething with jealousy over here."

He draped his arm around the back of the booth and she unconsciously inched closer to him. "There's no competition here." He twisted a lock of her hair around her finger, tugged on it playfully. "You're still my biggest fan, right?"

She lifted her eyes to his and nodded, wishing inside that he knew, that she had the courage to tell him, just how much of a fan she was.

He laid his hand against her cheek, and she felt his warm breath upon her lips. "And I'm yours."

Their lips melted together in quiet intensity, and everything else—their fear, their pasts and their uncertain future—disappeared.

Chapter 9

Alex leaned against the headboard and groaned in frustration. The feel of Cara's sweet lips on his own was still so real in his mind, so alive in his senses, that it was hard to believe she wasn't still in his arms, and in his bed.

Right or wrong, he had wanted to romance her tonight. Make her feel special. A fast car ride, great food and an amazing make-out session in the Porsche after they left the club all added up to an unforgettable night that ended too soon. When they arrived home, she claimed she was "exhausted" and went to her room.

Now, as he sat trying to focus on finishing his tune, he was afraid he'd offended her somehow, and he wondered exactly what she thought about the evening… and about him.

What she didn't know was that his need for her went beyond physical lust. He cared about her, what she felt, thought and needed, more deeply than he could have ever imagined.

He tapped a pencil against his head and stared at the wall, wishing he had X-ray vision, wondering if she was as awake, and as aroused, as he was.

His erection stirred as he remembered the feel of her slender arms around his neck, the luscious dip between her breasts, the small waist that fit perfectly in his hands.

It frightened him that he wanted Cara so much, not only in his bed, but in his life. There was only one day left. It wasn't enough time. What if he lost her forever?

She's already gone, man. You never stood a chance. You really think she wants to be with someone who can't read?

With a sigh of resignation, he shoved the pencil and manuscript paper to the floor and turned off the light.

Cara stared at the ceiling and trembled at the memory of his fingers brushing her hair away from her face like it was crafted of the finest silk. The heat of his gaze tracing her body, penetrating her clothes and making her wet with desire.

She couldn't believe the man who'd kissed her senseless that evening, in the club and in the car, was the same person who'd practically slammed the door in her face barely forty-eight hours earlier.

This evening, she'd learned that Alex was warm, caring and gentle. The kind of man she could fall in love with for a lifetime.

Thin streams of moonlight filtered through the blinds. It was after one o'clock in the morning. He was probably sleeping, and the night that was so magical to her was just a nice memory to him.

Her heart lurched. By this time tomorrow, she'd be back in Brooklyn, alone in her bed as usual. Her time with Alex would be over forever.

The only consolation in the pain was that her identity would be safe. Alex would never know about her father, or what he did for a living, although he'd come close to finding out tonight. Although she never talked about her personal life with her other students, she still felt guilty about not being completely honest.

As long as she kept the survival of Beacon House at the forefront of her mind, she would be okay. But she knew it wasn't going to be easy. When he was kissing and touching her like he couldn't get enough, it was too easy to cross the line, and too hard to go back.

She got out of bed, let her gown puddle to the floor. *Only one more night.*

It was about time that she gave Alex Dovington a personal wake-up call of the most pleasurable kind.

Cara padded barefoot to Alex's room, clad only in a lace thong. His door was ajar and she counted his slow, even breaths as she calmed her own. Thankfully, he was fast asleep.

Moonlight shone through the window and illuminated his body. The sheet, tossed loosely around his waist, made her yearn to rip it off to reveal the rest. But there was no need to rush. She had the rest of the night to enjoy him, and she planned on taking time to savor every inch.

Inhaling deeply, she tiptoed to the edge of his bed, lifted the covers and curved her body to his, her breasts and belly sinking into his warmth.

With the lightest touch she could muster, she traced her finger along the crevice between his shoulder blades, down his spine and back up to the base of his neck. Although he didn't say a word, his involuntary shudder resonated against her stomach and she knew he'd awakened.

She revered his skin, her tongue and lips tasting boldly as the place between her legs began to moisten and throb. She lifted one leg, placed it gently on his thigh. His muscles immediately stiffened, and the hair on his thigh tickled her flesh.

Alex suddenly ripped the sheet off and pulled her on top of him. Wrapping his fingers in her hair, he crushed his mouth to hers.

He tasted of warm spice, and she thirsted for more as his tongue led her in a tribal dance of sensual exploration.

So percussive were their lips upon each other's face and neck, undulating in perfect rhythm, always seeking and finding new skin to taste. Their tongues played and darted, licked and prodded, until they were both breathless.

Skin to skin, Cara's heart pounded with his as Alex cupped her face. No words were spoken, but the question of should they or shouldn't they make love was finally answered in the unadulterated desire they saw in each other's eyes.

The line in the sand had been erased by a tidal wave of passion neither of them understood but both accepted.

His erection, a hard, thick slab against her stomach, tempted her to take a peek. But she didn't, preferring to simply feel his flesh continue to grow and pulse against her skin.

She shivered as his hands slipped down her back, cupped her buttocks. He gripped hard, thrusting her into a gasp, which he smothered with a kiss as he dragged his finger in the narrow gap under the thong, discovering tender flesh. Eager to stroke and coddle, she yelped when he ripped the lacy fabric in half.

Unencumbered, his hands spread her legs a little wider. Sealing her lips to his, his mouth swallowed her moans as his fingers teased, tapping lightly on her sensitive pearl. She threw her head back and panted as his lips traveled over her collarbone.

When his lips found her breasts, she cried out as his mouth fastened on her one tight tip. Wrapping his arms around her waist, he gently rolled her over onto her back while sucking her nipple with immeasurable tenderness.

"You're so beautiful," he whispered, softly anchoring her breasts in his hands. His tongue moved like wildfire over one stiff peak to the other, over and over until she thought she'd go mad. Powerful sensations rushed through her body, and she clamped her legs together. It was too soon.

Her body, tight with desire, strained up toward his mouth when his tongue dipped into her belly button. Laying his cheek upon her abdomen, he released his hands from her breasts and stroked them down her thighs, easing them apart. Cupping her buttocks, he knelt and then gently lifted her to his waiting lips.

Alex kept his eyes on hers as he hovered there, inches away, hot breath on her skin, and she whimpered and twisted with yearning. His tongue flicked like a serpent's and she writhed in response and he tightened his hold. Then lips met flesh and he began to suck and lick her into another dimension.

She leaned up on her elbows. Watching him dip and dive his tongue increased the pleasure and the frenzy for both of them.

"Unh…mhhhh," she cried out, dropping her head back, her hair blanketing the pillows.

Twisting and bucking in his grasp, he brought her close, so close she thought she would pass out. She sank back into the bed, mewing with pleasure, and stretched out her hands to him.

The angles and curves of their bodies melded together in utter need. Alex wove his hand through her hair, brought her lips to his. Penetrated and claimed her as his own.

Oh, how good he felt inside her.

How delicious his mouth tasted.

How perfectly in rhythm they moved together.

He moaned as she wrapped her legs around his waist, urging him to go deeper, rock harder. The primal dance of their bodies thumped flesh upon flesh. Tempo increased, his hands tangled in her curly locks, his mouth never leaving hers. Both seeking, climbing and pleasuring each other without bounds.

"Ahh…lex," she moaned, arching her body into his as he probed her core, thrusting into that secret place that broke her in two.

Her inner flesh held him captive, pulsed and rippled, until soon his entire body stiffened. With a guttural cry, he exploded into her, releasing bright bursts of pleasure that brought tears to her eyes, and she clutched his tight buttocks and rocked to heaven with him.

Their lips, bruised and swollen from their lovemaking, continued to move and explore each other. Both desperately trying to stay in the moment, wishing they could stop time.

As the night ebbed away into morning, neither wanted the pleasure to end and their uncertain future to begin.

Chapter 10

Alex propped himself on one elbow and admired the beautiful creature lying asleep next to him. He loved mornings, but for the first time in his life, he wished the sun wouldn't rise. There was only one word to describe last night: glorious.

Never before had he felt such a sense of oneness with another woman. It was like Cara had been created for him and he was created for her. There was no way he would ever let her go.

In a few minutes, the entire room would brighten. He didn't want the sunlight to wake her before he had a chance to think. He'd never told a woman he was falling in love with her, and he didn't want to screw up.

Speaking his emotions verbally had always been difficult. Words could be rejected, thrown back at his face or used against him.

Words were also so…final.

If only he could play his saxophone, then he could

tell Cara his feelings through his music. That was one reason why he loved playing so much, he could express whatever his feelings were on the spot, through his horn.

He never would have dreamed something positive would come out of his illiteracy. Not only was he learning to read, but because of Cara, he was learning to feel without remorse and love without boundaries. He felt incredibly blessed to know her.

You can't have love without truth.

The thought sucker-punched him, and he lay back upon the pillow and let out a quiet breath.

Would she still care about him if she learned the truth about his past? He didn't think he could bear it if any feelings that she had for him turned into fear.

No, it was too risky, he decided. Things were still too fresh between them. Telling her now would end their relationship before it ever really began.

He turned and propped himself on his elbow again, allowing his eyes to rove her body. Lush, full breasts. A baby-got-back behind. Legs that shouldn't even be legal in the fifty states, much less the U.S. territories.

Her lips were parted slightly, inviting him to bring her home from dreamland. She was a sight to behold. Asleep or awake, he could simply not resist her.

He traced a finger down the tiny crease below her nose. Slowly he lowered his lips to hers and kissed her softly on each corner of mouth before moving to the middle. He nudged her lips open and she moaned as his tongue slipped inside.

Her arms wrapped around his neck, and he deepened the kiss, pleasuring the warmth inside her mouth. He broke their embrace for only a second, noting that her eyes were still closed but her lips curved into a smile.

Slipping under the cool sheets, his lips hungrily sought the underside of her breasts, and it pleased him enormously when her nipples stiffened immediately at the touch of his lips.

His erection was painfully hard and he wanted nothing more than to penetrate her warmth right now. But this wasn't about him, it was about Cara. And this time, when he entered her, he wanted to see her eyes.

He dragged his lips away from her breasts and cupped her face in his hands.

"Good morning," he murmured low into her ear. "How's my little night prowler?"

He kissed her eyelids, and when she opened them his heart dropped. He didn't see desire there. He saw regret.

He took his hands off her face. "What's wrong? Did I hurt you?"

She shook her head and seemed to struggle to form words.

"Cara, what's wrong! Talk to me!" His voice bounced off the walls, louder than he intended, but damn, she was scaring him.

He reached out to stroke her hair, and his heart lurched when she jerked away, her eyes as wide as saucers.

"I shouldn't be here," she whispered. "Oh, my God."

"What are you talking about?" He reached for her hand again just as she was about to leap from the bed. She tried to jerk her hand away, but he held tight. "No, you're not going anywhere until you tell me what's going on."

Her cheeks were flushed, making her even more beautiful. "Last night was a mistake! That's what's wrong," she yelled.

He felt like he'd been slapped.

"What?"

"You heard me. Last night never should have happened, Alex. We...I made a big mistake. Now let me go!"

She wrested away from him and started toward the door, but he leaped out of the bed and slammed it shut before she got there.

He tried not to be distracted by her nude body, but it was difficult.

"Wait a minute. You come into my room and seduce me, and now you're going to walk out just like that?"

She nodded and started to reach for the doorknob.

"Like hell you are!" He grabbed her hand, turned her around and pinned her to the wall as he smothered her lips with a kiss that was meant to pleasure them both and prove to him that the passion he felt from her last night wasn't a dream.

"Kissing you like this is a mistake?" he urged, his voice thick with longing for her.

Her body clung to his as he planted his mouth all over her face and neck before settling back on her lips again, his hard, naked length crushed painfully between them. Their tongues entangled hot and loose with the kind of passion lovers have the freedom to release and the freedom to deny.

She pushed him away again. This time he didn't resist.

"I can't do this. It's the last day we have together to finish the book. I can't teach you under these circumstances."

"Then why did you come into my room last night?" *Why did you make me fall in love with you?*

She wiped her mouth, her eyes blazing. "I—I don't

know. I can't explain it right now. All I know is that it can't…it won't happen ever again."

She covered her breasts with her hands. "Now if you'll excuse me, I want to shower and get dressed. I'll meet you downstairs in an hour so we can wrap this up."

Without another word, Cara opened the door and walked out.

Alex sank down onto the bed. His brain was trying to process a range of emotions—rejection, confusion, anger. But his heart felt only one thing: love.

As far as he was concerned, recess was over. He didn't know what kind of game Cara was playing, but he wasn't going to stop pursuing her until he won her heart.

What have I done?

Cara leaned against the wall sobbing quietly as hot water pelted her body like tiny whips.

For the second time in less than two days, she'd made a colossal mistake that hurt both of them. She wished that the immense ache in her heart could be whisked away down the drain as easily as her tears.

It wasn't supposed to happen this way, and she wasn't supposed to feel like this.

All she'd wanted to do was seduce Alex, to pretend that she was his lover for one night, to do something daring for once in her life.

But her little experiment had blown up in her face. The intended result never involved actually falling in love with him.

Yes, he was the most gorgeous man she'd ever known and yes, he had fulfilled her every fantasy last night. But loving him and desiring him was wrong when she had not been completely truthful with him from the very beginning.

It wasn't like she hadn't had ample opportunity to set the record straight. When Tommy had called her to hire her, she could have said that she couldn't possibly teach Alex for personal reasons.

Or even before she'd stepped over his Harlem threshold, it would have been appropriate to tell him who she really was—and give him the opportunity to tear up the contract in her face if he chose.

But she'd done neither. Instead, she chose deceit over decency, and now she'd destroyed something before it even had a chance to begin.

Alex was the only man who'd ever made her feel like she was the most beautiful woman on earth. To be desired by Alex was a wondrous thing, but to be loved by him, to be his alone, was a dream that could never be fulfilled.

Not if she wanted to keep Beacon House open.

There was no question in her mind that her loyalty to the Harlem community far outweighed her need to be in any romantic relationship. Helping people change their lives was what she lived for. Not love. Not heartbreak.

Even though she cared deeply for him, she couldn't let last night get in the way of her goal. Somehow she had to get them back on track before it was too late.

She only had a few hours to make sure he could read the children's book comfortably and with no errors. After today, if he still needed additional help, she would refer him to one of the other literacy centers in the city.

But how was she going to get through the next few hours and hide the way she felt about him? How would she get through a lifetime without loving him?

She squeezed her eyes shut at the dull ache in her heart, the settling-in-for-winter kind of hurt that wouldn't easily go away with chocolate, ice cream or an afternoon nap. It was the kind of ache and longing that could only be eased by the man you loved, loving you in return.

Did he love her? The answer to that question sparked both hope and fear. She'd always wanted a man like Alex to love, and to love her. He was gorgeous, intelligent and talented beyond measure. He would be a difficult man to forget, let alone her feelings for him.

She turned off the water, wrapped herself in a towel. She rubbed the steam from the glass and when she looked in the mirror, she saw a woman in love. One who could not possibly be with the man she adored, and the tears fell again.

Alex whistled as he expertly flipped pancakes on the griddle, hoping the delicious smell would entice Cara to emerge from her bedroom. No woman could resist his homemade, melt-in-your-mouth, write-home-to-your-momma flapjacks, complete with a side of bacon and fresh-squeezed orange juice.

What better way to discuss their future than over a hot breakfast?

She had to eat, and at some point she had to talk about what happened between them this morning. He deserved to know why she'd walked out, and he wouldn't take "no comment" for an answer. By the time they left for Harlem that evening, he had to have a fool-proof plan in place for seeing her again.

"What's all this?"

Alex turned at the sound of Cara's voice and smiled. The sweater she wore was his favorite shade of blue and accentuated her curves in the most distracting way.

Remember. Look, but don't touch.

"Breakfast, of course," he said, sliding the last of the pancakes onto a platter. "It's nearly ready. Why don't you have a seat?"

He couldn't help but notice her eyes, so vibrant and alert last evening, were now puffy and tired. It hurt him to think he was the cause of her tears, and made him all the more eager to make things right again between them.

He walked over to her and cupped her elbow to lead her to the table, but she jerked away.

"I'm not hungry," she mumbled.

He frowned, trying but not succeeding to hide his disappointment from his face. "You haven't eaten since we went to Idella's. And I don't know about you, but hot, steamy sex like we had the pleasure of experiencing last night always makes me hungry the next morning," he added, raising a brow.

She rolled her eyes. "I don't need to be reminded that you've been with other people, Alex."

He bit back a smile at the jealous tone in her voice. She still cared about him. What she didn't know was that none of those women could compete with Cara. They were his past. She was his future.

"I wasn't trying to remind you of anything," he assured her. "I was only stating a fact. Don't you want to get to know me?"

"Of course I do, but like you said yourself, there are some things that should be left unsaid."

"Agreed." He raised his right hand, voice booming. "Thou shalt not speak of past relationships." He could see that she was trying not to grin. "I'm sorry," he said, extending his hand. "Apology accepted?"

Their eyes locked in a battle of egos. She nodded, and when she placed her warm hand in his, it took everything in him not to pull her into his arms.

He released her hand and let out a breath. "Let's eat."

Cara eyed the huge spread of food. "You shouldn't have gone through all this trouble." She sat down, spreading a napkin across her lap. "This is a feast fit for a—"

"Queen," he interrupted, grinning.

Her cheeks reddened and she poured the coffee. "I don't know how you can think about eating, when we have so much to do today."

"Easy." He gulped down some juice. "I'm a guy."

She rolled her eyes. "That old excuse."

He watched, amused, as she stacked three pancakes, followed by four pieces of bacon on her plate.

"Um. For someone who said she wasn't hungry—" He tilted his head toward her plate. "I'm just sayin'!"

"And I'm just leaving," she retorted with a glare, and rose to get up from the table.

Alex burst out laughing and grabbed her hand. "Geez, Cara. It was a joke. Sit down and eat as much as you like."

They ate in silence for a while, and he wondered what she was thinking about, and if her thoughts had anything to do with him.

He was on his second pancake when he couldn't take the quiet any longer. "I made this breakfast special for you," he blurted out. "To thank you for all you've done for me this weekend."

He wiped his mouth, took her hand in his. "Around you, I'm not ashamed that I can't read. I'm not ashamed… to be me."

Her eyes were gentle. "Being illiterate is no reason to be ashamed."

"I know that now," he admitted, feeling the weight of a long-held burden lift off his chest. "And I couldn't have done it without you. I can't do it without you."

He paused, cleared his throat. "I want you to continue to be my teacher, for as long as it takes. What do you think?"

She took her hand from his and turned to look out the window, the sunlight dancing upon her corkscrew curls. He smiled at the memory of playing with her hair last night as she fell asleep in his arms.

Desire rolled through him again and he clenched his fist against it, then realized she hadn't said a word.

"Wow, you're awfully quiet. I hope that means you're thinking about all the wonderful ways you want to say yes to me."

She turned back and shook her head. "It wouldn't work, Alex."

"What are you talking about? We're a great team."

"Yes, but it's not that simple."

"Sure it is. All you have to do is open your mouth and say 'yes.'"

Her lip quivered. "Last night changed everything," she insisted, her tone unfriendly and professional. "We…I crossed a line that never should have been crossed. Severing ties is the only right thing to do."

He couldn't believe what he was hearing. He reached for her hand, and his heart clenched when she moved away and crossed her arms around her chest.

It hurt him to think she wanted to drop out of his life so easily after all they had shared this weekend, both emotionally and physically.

"Severing ties? It sounds like you want to cut off a

limb," he said, half joking. "All I'm asking is to continue the great work we've been doing."

"There are plenty of qualified literacy teachers in the city. As soon as we get home, I'll call Tommy and give him a couple of names to check out."

"So when Monday rolls around, we'll just go back to our lives, huh?"

She nodded, and seemed perfectly fine with the course their conversation was taking. "I'm sorry about last night. I truly don't know what came over me. All I do know is that I don't want it to happen again."

Alex cocked an eyebrow. "From the way you responded to my kisses this morning, I don't believe for a second that you don't want me to make love to you right now."

Cara pushed her chair away from the table and stood. "You're impossible, you know that?" she huffed. "Your ego continues to astound me. You don't know what I want, and if I have anything to say about it, you never will."

Alex gave her a smug grin. *We'll see about that.*

"Oh, my gosh," she gasped with a glance at the clock. "We have to get moving or else we'll never finish what I need to cover today."

At that moment, his phone rang out the melody to Charlie Parker's "Now's the Time."

"Saved by the bell," he said, and she rolled her eyes again.

"What's up, Tommy? Tonight? What time?" He listened for a moment, his eyes locked on Cara's curious gaze. "Yeah, I'll be there. Thanks, man."

He slipped his phone back into his pocket. "Well, I've got to cut the weekend short."

"Why, what happened?"

"I just got a call to play at Lincoln Center this evening. My driver will be here in an hour."

She stared at him, then shrugged. "No problem. We have a couple of hours in the car to study."

He shook his head, hid a smile. "I have to review the charts for the concert tonight. Tommy is sending them to my phone now. I have an app that lets me read them right on the screen."

Her face fell in disappointment, but he was delighted with the turn of events. "The book tour doesn't start till Friday. We have plenty of time between now and then to be sure that I'm ready for it."

"I have other clients who—" she protested.

He cut her off, his voice stern, but his heart was soft. "Teaching me to read in three days is what you were hired to do, wasn't it?"

"Of course, but…" she sputtered.

"But nothing," he insisted. "We both know I'm making great progress, but as you said yourself, I still need a little more work."

He hated what he was about to say, but he had to throw it out there and make his point clear.

"Besides, backing out now would mean that you haven't fulfilled your part of the deal, so obviously neither would I."

His words hung like dynamite in the air. She stared at him in astonishment, and he could tell by the look in her eyes that she was peeved at his threat.

"Of course, Mr. Dovington," she snapped. "I have every intention of completing the assignment to your satisfaction."

He couldn't help but smile, and admire her legs, when with a twirl of her skirt she spun on her heels and left the room.

He whistled as he cleaned up the kitchen. Thanks to fate and a phone call, the day was turning around in his favor.

Chapter 11

A rainy Monday morning, no umbrella, a broken heart and an eviction notice.

I love my life.

Cara stood in front of Beacon House in a virtual stupor. Maybe if she stared long enough at the legal paper of doom, which was already flapping in the wind, it would fly away.

But it didn't budge. Just like her hair, which was now plastered to her face because she'd been standing there so long. Finally, she tore the notice off and unlocked the door.

She walked down the short hallway to her office, slipped off her soppy raincoat, and sat down at her desk, hugging her arms to her body. The building was cold and drafty, but she was hesitant to turn on the heat so early in the season.

Reluctantly, she turned her attention to the eviction

notice. Her hands shook as she carefully read the fine print.

She had thirty days to vacate the premises. Thirty days to find a new location for Beacon House. One that was affordable for her and convenient for her clients.

Cara buried her face in her hands and fought back a fresh wave of tears. She was finished. There were simply no extra funds available. And there wasn't enough time to raise the money she would need to hire movers, let alone rent a place.

Beacon House would cease to exist by Halloween.

Her personal nightmare had begun and she couldn't see a way out. What was she going to do?

Sure, she could call her father, who in turn could make a few phone calls, and all of a sudden, the eviction notice would be retracted by her landlord with profuse apologies.

But she was never the type of daughter to go running to her daddy to solve her problems, and she wasn't going to start now. Even if he was one of the most influential people in New York. Even if it was mighty tempting right now to bow her head and listen to him tell her she should have been an attorney.

She wiped away her tears and yawned. She'd gotten herself into this mess, she'd just have to figure a way out, even though she was so exhausted she could barely move. Alex continued to haunt her thoughts, and last night she had barely slept.

She didn't like that what she'd come to do that weekend was not complete. She'd signed a contract to teach him to read, not fall in love with him. That she would have to see him again didn't make her happy at all. If anything, it made her sad, because it would only prolong what would be an inevitable forever goodbye.

The ride home was as excruciating as she expected. Neither of them spoke much and that was bad enough. The crackle of desire was still there, but there was the undeniable sense that again something had shifted between them.

Alex didn't appear to be affected a great deal one way or another. Once they got in the car, he immediately pulled out his phone and was engrossed in the charts he had to learn. Cara wondered if he even knew she was in the same car with him.

Did he even remember that a few hours before, they were feverishly pleasuring each other in ways she would never forget? Did he even care?

He did seem surprised when she insisted he drop her off in front of Beacon House instead of her apartment. Sometimes her father liked to make unannounced visits to her home. She didn't want to take the chance of running into him.

She'd hoped he would kiss her goodbye, but all she got when she stepped out of the limo was her bags, a polite handshake and a heart filled with pain. It seemed he'd forgotten to pack caring and concern alongside his socks. A classic symptom of the he's-just-not-that-into-you disease.

Then his limo pulled away and she watched it weave through traffic until it was out of sight.

The pain of his rejection seared through her heart anew, and she sighed. It was time to deal with something that could destroy her credit, but not her heart. Accounts Payable.

She was booting up her computer when her office manager popped in the room. "Good morning!"

Cara jumped out of her chair and stretched across

the desk to snatch up the eviction notice she'd left on the corner in plain sight.

"What's that you have there?"

Nancy was in her mid-fifties with the eyes of a hawk, ears of a cat and a heart of gold.

She grasped the document, slid back into her chair. "Oh, nothing."

At Nancy's raised eyebrow, she burst out crying. "Oh, everything!" She handed her the paper. "I don't know what I'm going to do."

Nancy's expression soured and Cara felt even worse. As owner of Beacon House, she was supposed to provide a stable work environment for her employees. Soon they would both be dusting off their resumes.

"I'm sorry. I'm sure you know what this means."

"That you're not giving up?" Nancy pulled up a chair and sat down. "Because I truly hope you are not."

Cara gave her a wan smile. "I don't know if I have anything left to give."

"Hmm. Well, I've learned that sometimes at your lowest point the greatest things can happen."

"I am at my lowest point." Cara looked all around and smirked. "And nope, nothing's happening."

"Give it some time. I bet the answer to your prayers will come walking through the door when you least expect it."

Cara remained silent and fought the urge to roll her eyes. Although she knew she meant well, Nancy was forever waxing philosophical. Like all the world's problems could be solved with a sound byte.

The only thing she'd like to see walking through the door was a gigantic check with Beacon House and tons of zeros written all over it.

Now *that* would be answered prayer.

Nancy rose and stretched. "I better go crank up my own computer and check voice mail. You have back-to-back clients this morning. Mr. Hernandez is your first. Did you remember to bring your smelling salts?"

Cara groaned. Gabe Hernandez was an eighty-year-old man who ate a clove of garlic and drank a shot of whiskey every morning. He claimed they were the secret to his longevity, but they smelled like death to her.

When Nancy closed the door, Cara navigated to the computer file containing all her financial information. She picked up the phone to dial her attorney.

It was going to be a very long and busy day, but time and tasks were exactly what she needed to try to forget Alex Dovington.

Alex squeezed into the A train, jam-packed with folks wishing they were anywhere but on a crowded subway, including him. He was on his way to a friendly showdown with Cara, and he aimed to win.

He probably should have called ahead, but surprising her meant she couldn't run away. That was good, because what he had to ask her could change both of their lives.

He'd just gotten out of a meeting with his public relations manager. Although he made a halfhearted attempt to cancel it, the book tour was a go and it was less than four days away.

His insides quaked with fear, not ready to deal with the publicity and the likelihood that he was going to make a complete fool of himself. He had to do everything in his power to ensure that he and Cara spent as much time together as possible, so that he could prepare for what might be the most embarrassing day of his life.

The entire ride home he had hoped Cara would insist, in her own way, that they continue with the lessons. That she would pull him away from the charts that he already knew backward and forward. But the only time she spoke to him was to decline his invitation to attend his gig at Lincoln Center.

She was a consummate professional and educator, but what did that have to do with their feelings for one another?

While he didn't know the extent of her emotions for him, the sinking feeling that she was hiding something from him was getting stronger. And he didn't like it one bit.

He hoped that tonight he could put his reservations to rest.

At 125th Street, he emerged from the subway with a throng of fellow riders. When he arrived at her office, only a few blocks away, his heart swelled with pride. Located in between two vacant storefronts, Beacon House was literally a diamond in the rough. He admired the gold lettering on the glass and the window boxes filled with yellow and lavender flowers.

He rang the buzzer a couple of times, and when she finally opened the door, her hair and her expression were frazzled.

"What are you doing here, Alex?" Her frustration was palpable, and his heart went out to her.

He smiled. "Is that anyway to talk to your favorite student?"

Her lips were set in a thin line. "I was getting ready to leave."

He pumped his fist. "Perfect timing! You can join me for dinner at my place, and after that, you can continue with the lessons you owe me."

With a sniff, she folded her arms across her chest.

"Is that an order? I guess you're not into asking either, just telling."

She turned and walked away from him, as fast as her tight legs could go. He followed, grinning. At least she was talking to him. He caught up and grabbed her elbow.

Turning her around to face him, he looked into her eyes.

"I'm sorry. That came out wrong. Dinner. Then will you teach me tonight? That is, if you don't have any other plans."

And if you do, it better not be with another man.

She stepped away, but he wrapped his arm around her waist and pulled her close.

His hazel eyes searched her brown ones, saw confusion. She was clearly on the fence about him, but why? Especially when she had so much at stake. He had to find out.

"Please?"

She bit her lip in a way that made his groin tighten. At that moment, he wanted nothing more than to crush her against the wall and taste the place where her teeth made contact with her flesh. But now was not the time.

His grip on her waist loosened and she stepped aside.

"Okay, I'll have dinner with you. But no lesson. Unfortunately, I left the book at home."

"No problem, we can just cab over there and pick it up."

"No!" she exclaimed.

Pain stabbed his heart. This was the second time she refused to let him come to her house. Was there another man in her life?

Cara cleared her throat. "I'll bring in the book tomorrow. Call me in the morning and make an appointment.

Tuesdays are fairly light, so I can probably squeeze you in."

Make an appointment? Squeeze him in? She was really trying his patience.

He shrugged, trying not to show his annoyance. "Sure, whatever you think is best. Ready to head out?"

She nodded. "I just need to gather my things."

He walked into the small waiting room and smiled at the poster featuring Uncle Sam pointing a gnarled finger, declaring "We Want You to Read!"

Minutes later, they stepped outside and she locked the door.

He gestured toward the building with admiration. "You should be proud of yourself, Cara. You're doing great things for the community. I hope you'll be able to continue here for many years to come."

She looked at him, her eyes moist, and he got the feeling she was in trouble, but he didn't want to push her to talk about it.

"Do you mind if we walk?" she asked.

"Not at all, it's only a few blocks."

They fell silent, succumbing to their thoughts and the sounds of rush hour traffic. They arrived at Alex's town house just as it was starting to rain again. He took her coat, hung it in the closet and was escorting her to the kitchen when the doorbell rang.

"I hate to put you to work, but would you mind setting the table while I go see who's at the door?"

Cara agreed and began to search the kitchen for the plates and glasses.

"Dinner is served," announced Alex a few minutes later.

She gaped at the two large paper bags he was carrying, and her face lit up. "You ordered from Sylvia's?"

A soul-food institution, Sylvia's had been serving traditional Southern cuisine in Harlem for over thirty-five years.

"The one and only!" He began unloading plastic containers onto the counter. "I've got chicken, ribs, greens, macaroni and cheese, buttered biscuits, sweet tea and for dessert, pecan pie."

"Why didn't you tell me that in the first place? I wouldn't have hesitated before accepting your invitation."

They laughed as they filled their plates, then sat down to eat in silence.

Later, Cara pushed her plate away. "Delicious, but I'll be paying for it on the scale tomorrow." She sipped her tea. "I read the reviews in the *New York Times*. Sounds like you had a great show last night, congratulations."

Alex swallowed and nodded. "Everything was perfect, except for one thing."

"What's that?"

He pointed his fork at her. "You weren't there."

She looked uncomfortable. "I had to…"

"…pick up your cat, I know," he said dryly. "Anyway, I would have loved to see you in the audience. Don't worry. I'll find a way for you to make it up to me. But first, I want to show you something."

Alex cleared their plates, then went into the living room and carefully took his Grammy Award out of its case. He returned to the kitchen and handed it to Cara.

"Here. I want you to hold it."

Her eyes widened and she gave him a questioning look.

"Seriously, it's okay." He gently placed the award in her cupped hands.

"It's so heavy!" she said in awe.

"That's because of all the blood, sweat and tears that go into winning one of these things," he joked.

He watched her intently. "You know, you're the first person I've ever let touch, let alone hold my Grammy."

"Really? Why me?"

He shrugged. "Because I believe you understand the sacrifices it takes to make your dreams come true."

She nodded in agreement. "You give up a lot, sometimes more than you realize at the time."

"And when you make it, when you achieve what you've wanted since you were a kid, you wonder, that's it? What do I do now?" He paused. "That's where I'm at, Cara."

He took the Grammy back. "I don't know if I want this anymore."

Even as he spoke the words, he couldn't believe he was saying them. But at the same time, an overwhelming sense of relief filled him. It felt good to admit his feelings to someone who cared about him, instead of always hiding behind his public persona.

Her caring about him was one thing he could depend on. It felt great because it was real. He knew that she cared about him, not his money or his status.

She looked at the award, then back at him. "Are you saying you want to get out of the music business?"

He gripped it tighter. "Maybe."

Her voice held no disdain, only curiosity. "Why?"

Alex set the Grammy down on the kitchen counter. How much should he tell her? He wanted to put his trust in her completely, but there was still that nagging feeling that she was hiding something from him.

"There are things you don't know about me, Cara." He sighed. "If I could turn back time I wouldn't even have this Grammy, my town house or anything else for that matter."

"Remember what you said, everything happens for a reason."

"No!" He slammed his fist down on the counter. "Everything doesn't happen for a reason. Things happen as a result of the choices we make. Choices we learn to regret, when it's too late."

He turned away, embarrassed at his outburst. When he felt her presence next to him and her warm hand on his arm, the lump in his throat grew larger.

"Everyone deserves a second chance, Alex. No matter what."

He faced her and she didn't move, their bodies inches away from each other. Lifting one curl of her hair, he spiraled it around his finger, then let go.

"Do you really believe that?" he asked, searching her eyes.

She nodded, her lips quavering. "Yes."

Thank you, Lord.

Her response was music to his ears. It meant that when the day came for him to tell her the truth about his past, she would likely be more open and accepting.

That day was coming soon. He threaded his fingers through her hair. He was falling in love with her, and he knew that keeping secrets would destroy any hope for a future with her.

He closed the gap between them, felt her body tremble when he cupped her chin and gently traced his thumb along the back of her neck. She bent her head back slightly and her long hair tickled his arm.

"If you show me where it is, I'll make us some coffee," she whispered, moving away in an attempt to interrupt his romantic gesture.

Alex blocked her by putting his other hand on the counter, and stepped even closer. When he drew her body to his, he hardened immediately at the sound of her gasp.

A soft moan escaped her lips as he pushed her hair behind her shoulder, then drew a finger along the sensitive folds of the outside of her ear.

"What do you like in your coffee? Cream or sugar?" she said, her breath quickening as he tickled her earlobe.

He placed his hands gently on the sides of her face and looked deeply into her eyes, trying to convey all that he was beginning to feel for her, even though he knew it was impossible.

"Both."

His kiss was light as he pressed into her lips. They tasted of sugar and sweet tea, and he wanted to devour them. But he held back until she slipped her arms around his neck and kissed him back with an urgency that surprised them both.

She parted her lips and accepted his tongue, and he groaned involuntarily. He sunk into the warm cavern of her mouth, drinking in her essence, always wanting more.

His flesh throbbed against her hard abdomen in desperate and painful need as her fingers roved his back, as if on a hunt for buried treasure. His muscles twitched in response to her sensuous touch, and she tore herself away from him, her eyes wide.

"Alex, we need to slow down," she breathed, her face flushed.

He tried to kiss her again, but she scooted away and walked out of the kitchen.

Alex's legs were unsteady as he followed her. "Why does it always seem like you are running away from me?"

Cara grabbed her raincoat from the closet and shoved her arms into it. "I'm not running away. I've had a long day today and I'm tired. I need to go home. Thank you so much for dinner. It was fantastic."

She grabbed the door handle, and Alex put his hand over hers. "We need to talk about this, Cara. And soon."

"We will, I promise," she said, seeming nervous. "Call me tomorrow and we'll set up a time to go over the book once more."

"I'm sorry, I can't. I'll be in the studio all day recording. I guess you're going to have to come to me."

"I have to check my schedule."

Since when did he become just an appointment slot, he thought, his temper flaring, yet his determination and desire for her remained steady.

He kept his voice firm. "Find the time. There's only two more days to the tour. I'll text you the address."

She nodded and they stepped outside. He hailed a cab and before she got in, he kissed her cheek.

"See you tomorrow. And this time, don't forget the book, and your pretty smile."

The cab lurched away and he pumped his fist in the air, happy that Cara agreed to meet him at the studio.

Not that she had much choice.

Before the donation check could be written to Beacon House, she had to fulfill the contract terms and finish teaching him how to read.

His part of the deal was to open her eyes to the fact that she was falling in love with him before she walked out of his life forever.

Chapter 12

The next morning, Cara stepped off the subway platform at 28th Street and Lexington Avenue with one goal: to say goodbye to Alex forever.

She knew it definitely wouldn't be easy to walk away from a man she'd wanted for longer than she cared to remember. But it was the only way to protect both of them from getting hurt.

The October air was crisp and cool as she walked to the recording studio a few blocks away. People hurried by feeding on the upbeat, infectious energy that was the spirit of New York City. Rush hour in New York occurred 24 hours a day, 365 days a week, and normally she found it uplifting, even soothing.

But today, her feet dragged and her mood right along with it. She'd finally found the love of her life and now she had to give him up. All because of her father, and a little thing called fear of commitment.

Put the two together and she was on a one-way trip to perpetual singleness.

The unfairness of it all made her want to do something inane like shake her fist at the sky. But with her luck, she'd probably get struck by lightning.

The kisses they'd shared last night resonated through her mind. His lips, full and warm, were so insistent to claim her again as his own she felt she would drown. He had restored emotions and spine-tingling feelings that she'd thought were long dead. In his arms, she felt amazingly alive.

The studio was located in a nondescript building with no sign. Wary, she pressed a button and someone buzzed her in. She stood in the foyer, clutching her briefcase and purse, not knowing what to do next.

She jumped at the sound of Alex's booming voice. "Cara, we're down in the basement. Come on down and watch your step!"

She walked to the end of the hall, and she and her two-inch heels started to navigate down the stairs.

They almost made it the whole way.

"Whoa!" Alex grabbed her by both elbows just before she fell flat on her face. "Easy there!"

"Special delivery," she joked, as her briefcase and purse flew off her shoulder and thumped to the floor. "You're always in the right place at the time I make a complete fool of myself."

"It's exactly where I want to be." He searched her eyes, and she was touched by the concern in his voice. "Seriously, are you okay?"

Her face heated and she moved out of his grasp as politely as she could. "Yes, although I'm a complete klutz sometimes, if you haven't noticed."

"I think it's kind of cute," he intoned, handing her things to her.

"I think it's kind of dangerous." She smirked, testing her ankle for a sprain.

"Not if I'm always here to save you." He smiled at her as if he wanted a response, but she didn't have one.

Taking her hand, he led her into a room filled with expensive-looking equipment and walled with a gray, spongy material that looked like honeycombs.

"Cara, I'd like you to meet Richie Adams, he's the best sound engineer in the business. He's also the owner, so be nice to him," he joked.

"Don't listen to him," said Richie as he shook hands with Cara. "He's just trying to butter me up so I'll give him more recording time for free."

Everyone laughed. "I hear you're going to be helping us out on the session today," said Richie.

Cara shot Alex a questioning look.

"I'll explain in a minute," he said soothingly, his voice caressing her ear.

Alex turned to Richie. "Hey, man, we'll be ready soon."

"The clock is running right into my bank account," said Richie, tapping his watch. "So take your time. It's all good!"

Alex laughed and the two men high-fived before he led her into another room that could only be described as a "man cave." There was a large flat-screen TV muted to ESPN, a black leather sectional, a small bar and a pool table. The walls were covered with musicians like Jimi Hendrix, John Coltrane and, oddly enough, Liberace.

She set her briefcase and purse on the couch and

pointed at the picture of the deceased eccentric pianist who had dominated Las Vegas in the 1970s.

"That's Ritchie's personal favorite," said Alex. "Don't ask!"

"Trust me, I won't." She put her hands on her hips. "So, what's going on, Alex? I thought you wanted me to come here so we can review the book."

"We'll get to that, but I need you to do me a favor first."

Her eyes narrowed. "What is it?"

"I want you to sing the lyrics you composed for my song."

Her mouth gaped, stunned by what he was asking her. "Why?" she stammered, pulse racing.

"It's for a sound check. Richie got some new equipment in the studio that I've never recorded with before and I want to check levels. I need to make sure everything works properly."

Her voice wavered. "You mean you want me to…"

"Sing," Alex finished for her. "You just need to lay down one track, that's it, okay?"

"Alex, I don't think…" Her voice trailed off.

If she had known Alex would be planning this, she would never have agreed to meet him at the studio. The man was full of surprises.

He gave her shoulders a reassuring squeeze. "Don't worry. Nobody will hear you but me and Richie."

She regarded him thoughtfully, dressed in a cream-colored Cuban-style shirt and black trousers that accentuated his handsome build. It was so hard to say no to him. Especially when he looked off-the-charts sexy.

There was so much of him waiting to be explored. But none of it was possible anymore. She was too busy keeping it real—professional, that is, too afraid to be anything more than his literacy teacher.

"What do you say, Cara? Will you sing?" He lifted her hand and kissed it. His lips felt warm and lush, and the tenderness of his touch spiraled through her body. "For me?"

Blushing from all his attention, she nodded.

His smile lit up her entire world. "Thank you."

Wrapping her hand in his, he led her to the little studio. "Make yourself comfortable."

She sat down on the wooden stool and he adjusted the microphone to her lips. He gave her a set of headphones and placed them over her ears.

She was shocked when he handed her the lyrics she'd sung to his ballad. "But…I—"

He touched his finger to her lips. "Hush. You can do this. Just pretend you're in my shower again."

"I'll let you know when we're ready. Sit tight." He kissed her forehead and left the room.

A few minutes later, she heard Alex's voice through her headphones. "Nod when you hear the instrumental in your right ear." A few seconds later, she heard the piano, bass and drums through her headphones. She nodded.

"Okay. Now just lay down the vocal track right over it. Nice and easy." He smiled at her through the glass. "Ready when you are."

She took a deep breath, closed her eyes and began to sing.

It's tearing me apart
To give you a chance
Still I'd sell
My soul for you

And now that you are here
I can't understand
Why you ever
Left me
Now is the time for you and me
To take a chance on love
Don't wait to see
Now is the time for us.

When she finished, Alex asked her to do it again, then three more times. She was trying hard to be patient, but how long did it take to check levels?

He came in and hugged her. "Great job, thank you. We're done."

"I'm glad I could help, but do you still have time to review the book? I have to leave soon."

"Of course," he said. "That's why I invited you here originally. I appreciate you making time in your schedule."

When they got back to the man cave, Cara headed straight for her briefcase.

"Oh, no!" she cried.

Alex strode over to her in alarm. "What's wrong?"

Cara was so angry at herself she almost burst out crying. "The book. I left it at home," her voice broke. "I can't believe this is happening."

She racked her brain trying to figure out what happened, and then it hit her. She had two briefcases, both black leather, and the one with the book in it was at home, probably being used as a bed by her cat, Molly.

How could she have been so careless?

"It's okay, Cara. Can you drop by my house later tonight?"

She swallowed a frustrated scream, then nodded. What other choice did she have?

She picked up her briefcase and purse. "I have other clients waiting so I better get going."

Alex touched her elbow. "Thanks again."

She gave him a faint smile. "I'll see myself out."

She turned and walked down the hall as fast as her heels could carry her. She didn't want to say goodbye to Alex, but she had no choice. Waiting another day, another moment, would only make it hurt more. By the time she got onto Lexington Avenue, tears of frustration and longing were streaming down her face.

Cara's hands trembled as she pressed Alex's doorbell. She couldn't believe that only five days earlier she'd stood in the very same spot, unsure if she could complete this insane assignment. In a few hours, the task of teaching Alex how to read in time for the book tour would be complete. And her secret would remain hidden.

Both outcomes were what she'd hoped for, prayed for. Then why did she feel so sad?

She slumped against the doorway, knowing the reason, but choosing not to fully accept it. Despite her best efforts, she'd fallen in love with Alex.

The man she'd admired from afar for years had become part of her every thought. His commanding presence remained with her, haunting her dreams, invading her present.

The desire she felt for him was always there, simmering below the surface, ready to erupt at any moment. With him, she was uninhibited, wanton and sensual. And she wanted nothing more than to be with him forever.

But what scared her the most was that he wanted her, too. She could feel it in his touch, the desire in his eyes, the warmth of his arms and his concern for her well-being.

Everything was wonderful now, but how would things be in one month or one year? Would he still feel the same way about her? Was Harlem's most eligible bachelor ready to settle down, too?

She straightened and nervously touched the back of her hair, which she'd wrestled into a neat chignon.

The question of whether he was or was not ready for a relationship with her was moot. He had every reason to hate her father, and when he found out she'd been lying to him, he would hate her, too. And that would be the end of any feelings he had for her.

She wanted to bolt, but she pressed the doorbell again, half hoping he wasn't home.

The door opened and her breath caught in her throat. She'd never known any man who could make her wet with desire just at the mere sight of him. He wore a cream button-down shirt with the sleeves rolled up and gray trousers. Even his bare feet were sexy.

He clasped her hand in his and drew her through the doorway while she discreetly inhaled the spicy scent of his cologne. "I'm glad you were able to make it. Come on in."

He helped her with her coat, his fingers brushing against the back of her bare neck, sending tiny tremors down her spine.

When she faced him again, her face grew hot as his eyes seared her body, clad in a navy wraparound dress that was simple but elegant.

"You look beautiful."

His baritone voice caressed her with admiration, and

she knew she would replay his compliment in her mind over and over.

He took her elbow. "How was the rest of your day?"

"Busy," she replied. "I had a full afternoon of clients, so I didn't get any paperwork done. I brought it home. Hopefully, we'll finish early enough that I can get it done before bed."

He nodded. "I think if we run through the book a few times, I'll be okay. I can't believe the tour starts in less than two days."

"Time flies." *When you're falling in love.*

They entered the kitchen and Cara gasped in surprise. On the counter were votive candles, two glasses, a bottle of wine and a small platter of assorted cheeses and fruits.

"I hope you don't mind. Will you share some with me?"

She bit her lip. "Sure, I'd love a glass of wine. But only one, I do have to work tonight," she warned.

"I understand."

Cara hopped onto the bar stool and crossed her legs. Her dress got caught on the edge, revealing her bare thigh. Swooping it closed, she looked up and caught him watching her. Their eyes met and her throat went dry as he handed her a glass of wine.

He sat across from her and moved his chair closer until their knees almost touched. "I know our time together is about to end, and I just wanted to thank you again for all you've done for me."

The sincerity in his voice wound into her heart, and she blinked back tears. "Alex, I should be the one thanking you. Your donation is going to help so many people overcome illiteracy. I only wish you knew the impact you're going to have on their lives."

Per the contract, she should receive the donation by the end of the week. However, with the eviction pending, it would no longer be enough to save Beacon House from closure. But that was her problem, not his.

He shook his head. "No, I'm only giving money. You give yourself, every day, for your students. You truly are making the world a better place."

"I don't know about all that," she said, humbled. "But I hope I'm making a difference."

"You sure made a difference in my life." He sipped his wine. "I'll admit I was a little resistant at first."

Cara raised an eyebrow and coughed.

"Okay, okay." He laughed, held up a hand. "I was a lot resistant—to you, to learning to read, this whole book tour idea."

"But you came through on the other side. Be proud of yourself!"

"Never would have happened without you," he insisted, clinking his glass to hers. "You're an amazing woman, Cara."

His compliment made her heart glow anew. He held her gaze as they sipped their wine.

Her eyes darted to the digital clock on the stove and she put down her wineglass. "I hate to break up the party, but we better start or time will get away from us again."

His look said "would that be so bad?" but she held her ground and opened up the book on the counter.

"Why don't you read it all the way through first without stopping? Then we'll go back and address any words or phrases that give you trouble."

His voice sounded tentative at first but got stronger as he went along. Her heart swelled with pride as he read. He'd come such a long way, but he had a lot further to go. It saddened her to think that she wouldn't be the one to accompany him on his journey to functional literacy.

When Alex finished, Cara clapped as loudly as she could.

"That was fantastic! Great job!"

He blew out a breath. "I feel like I've benched about 300 pounds. I never knew words could beat a person up like that. No wonder Oscar was always a grouch."

She cracked up. "I never thought about it that way. I thought he was mean because he lived in a garbage can, but maybe he was just trying to escape."

"There is no escape from words," said Alex. "They can hurt, kill spirits and start wars."

She nodded. "They can heal, show love, inspire change, make someone laugh."

He reached over and touched her cheek. "And they can make someone never want to say goodbye."

Fear and choices hung like invisible tightwires between them. However, unlike at the circus, there was no safety net to break their fall. Only pain, uncertainty and secrets. At that moment, neither had the courage to take a step into the unknown.

I don't want to say goodbye, either.

Those were the words she wished she could say. Instead, she cleared her throat and closed the book. "I think you'll be fine on Friday."

"Will you be there?"

She shook her head. "No, I wasn't planning on it, and I have some pretty important meetings that day."

He sat back, an air of defeat surrounding him. "Oh, I was hoping you would be."

Her heart lurched at the disappointment in his voice.

"It's getting late. I'd better head home. I'll email you some names of other literacy teachers."

Alex placed a hand on her knee, his eyes twinkling as he got off the chair. "Wait, I have something I want to give you."

He reached into a cupboard and took out a notebook-size package wrapped in brown paper.

She stood up and went to his side. "What is it?"

"Open it and see, silly!"

She took the package and opened it with care. When she saw what it was, she couldn't believe her eyes.

Framed and mounted was his tune, the one she'd stolen. The song that almost broke them apart now had finally brought them together.

He'd forgiven her.

His gentle eyes caressed her face. "Since you're my biggest fan, I thought you'd like to have it."

"Alex." Her eyes filled with tears and she gazed up at him. "I was so surprised when you asked me to sing it this morning, and now this…gift? I don't know what to say."

"Then let me say it for you." He palmed her face, lowered his lips to hers and treated her to a long and unforgettable kiss.

"Do you have anything else you want to say?" he asked.

Without a second thought, she flattened her hands against his neck, pulled him to her and kissed him long and deep. His mouth was so warm and wonderful, so insistent about her own, that time and the work waiting for her back home were forgotten.

Her body went slack and he linked his arm around her waist, pulling her close. Her fears were wrestled to the ground by his eager mouth and tongue, teasing and taunting her with more pleasure to come.

He leaned her against the table and kissed her nose and her eyelids and grazed her brows with his lips. She loved the feel of his hands clutched around her waist, his hard length imprisoned between them.

Trailing a finger from the bridge of her nose, she bit the tip in mock protest and he smiled.

"Close your eyes," he muttered against her ear, breath ragged. "I have something else to show you."

She laughed. "What do you have up your sleeve now?"

"You'll see. Lights out."

Giggling, she squeezed her eyes shut as he grabbed her hand and led her forward a short distance.

"Okay. You can open up," he said, letting go of her hand.

She blinked in disbelief at the sight before her.

Hundreds of pink and red rose petals blanketed the heavy oak dining table, and right in the center was a Scrabble board.

Cara walked up to it and read the words formed by the little wooden letters:

I LOVE YOU

Tears streamed down her face as Alex stood behind her and wrapped his arms around her waist.

"This is my love letter to you." He twirled her around to face him. "I learned how to read a lot of words over the past few days, but these are the only ones that matter."

He tilted her chin up with the pad of his thumb. "I love you, Cara."

The candles seemed to cheer from every corner of the room as he kissed her tears away. Cara curled into his embrace and succumbed to his kiss fully and completely, drowning in the delicious flavor of his lips, so tempting to bite and lick.

His mouth tasted of wine, and as she stroked her hands up his neck and over the smooth skin of his head, a moan arose from deep within his throat.

The heat of Alex's body invaded her own as her lips parted to take his tongue deeper into her mouth, allowing him to explore her at will.

She murmured low in her throat and he responded by crushing her body against him. Swaying from side to side, she longed to touch and stroke the hard flesh that poked the thin fabric of her dress.

He groaned again, broke the kiss and kept his gaze on hers as he trailed his finger down her chin, the length of her neck.

Slowly he traced the swell of her cleavage, taking a dip into the skin between her breasts as if he only wanted a taste. His fingertips raked lightly across her nipples, and they popped alive from his touch. Her mouth watered remembering the feel of his lips around them.

As if he could read her mind, he traced the curves of her waist and fumbled with the single tie that held her dress together.

Growing impatient, she tried to untie it herself, but he batted her hand away and scolded her by rubbing the pads of his thumbs against her nipples in a circular motion so slow that she felt her knees collapse against him.

Finally, he untied her dress and slid it off her shoulders. He stepped back and she heard him suck in a breath at the sight of her body, now clad in only a lace bra and thong.

With a shy smile on her lips, she reached up and released her hair from the chignon, enjoying seeing his desire for her burn even brighter in his eyes.

She met his gaze and almost laughed aloud when he started unbuttoning his shirt a lot quicker than he'd untied her dress.

She stepped toward him and peppered his neck with slow, sensual kisses as he slid his hands over her buttocks. He squeezed her to him and she cried out when he suddenly lifted her and laid her gently on the table.

The scent of roses wafted around her and provided a velvety texture against the table's hard wood. The square game pieces felt cool against the small of her back, and instead of hurting, they felt amazingly good, heightening her desire.

He leaned over and buried his head in her neck, nuzzling her with tiny kisses. She twisted and moaned when his tongue discovered a sensitive spot and lingered there until she pushed his head away.

He unbuckled his pants and slipped off his boxers. Her mouth watered at the sight of his beautiful body fully exposed to her. He was powerfully built, and there was a sheer layer of sweat contoured over his muscled skin.

At that moment, she wanted him inside her more than anything. Her heart pounded in her chest as she lifted her arms and reached for him, but he caught her wrist in his hand.

"Not yet," he commanded. "I want to look at you."

Slowly he undid the front clasp of her bra, releasing her breasts to his eager eyes and hot tongue. He took his time, kneading and pleasuring and licking until her whimpers became raging gasps. Then he hooked his thumbs in the straps of her thong and planted little kisses all the way down her legs as he eased her underwear off.

He caressed every inch of her body, fire raging in his eyes, leaving her skin tingling with overwhelming physical need. His hands palmed her breasts, barely touching them, before he bent his mouth to each nipple and flicked the stiff tips again with tender abandon.

She threw her head back and his mouth came crushing back down to nuzzle at her neck.

"Cara," he breathed, as he lightly bit, then sucked her earlobe. "You have no idea what you do to me, woman."

She grew even wetter at the sensuality of his words, the natural juice of her need preparing her body to accept him.

Instinctively, she spread her legs and he slid a finger to explore her moist folds and the dark cavern she offered to him freely, lovingly. His tongue played on her flesh, and she squirmed with pleasure, game pieces digging into her back, arms and shoulders.

He stood up and her eyes landed on the hard length of flesh that jutted from his torso. Again, she reached for him. But he stepped back, picked up a handful of roses and let them drift like snowflakes. She closed her eyes as they landed softly on her body. Little petals of soft fire.

"Tell me you want me."

She opened her eyes, and met his. "Let your teacher show you instead," she whispered low.

His flesh was hot and hard as she tenderly stroked him, loved him with the palm of her hand, and when he could take her touch no more, he arched his shoulders back and eased into her lips with a groan. He was exquisite fullness in her mouth, on her tongue, in her grip.

When she broke contact, he pushed her back on the

table and with one swift motion pinned her arms above her head. Lifting her buttocks and pulling her toward him, he plunged his entire length into her body. She cried out and he silenced her by sucking on her bottom lip as he began to master her senses with deliciously slow movements.

She writhed in sensuous agony as his thumbs massaged her taut nipples. Shrieking with pleasure when he completely filled her, she begged him to come back to her when he teased and dragged his hard length against her moist flesh.

The scent of roses wafted in the air as he branded her body as his own, on his own terms. She was barely aware of the table creaking back and forth beneath them as he tugged her closer, delving deeper and deeper into her most private place.

She knew, then and there, that she belonged to him.

"Ohh!" She held her legs sky high as he thrust her into a sensual abyss, and she was falling and screaming out his name when she climbed again, taking him with her now, her lover man, as spasms of pleasure rippled through her body and exploded into his, and he gave her the gift of himself.

Uninhibited release.

Undeniable love.

Their hearts beat together in a rhythmic melody of mutual satisfaction as they lay together, rose petals and game pieces stuck to their bodies.

He brushed the hair from her face. "I love you, Cara. Don't leave," he muttered against her ear, breath ragged. "Stay with me tonight. Stay with me forever."

Tears filled her eyes. His words were so beautiful, but believing them would mean she would have to tell him the ugly truth. Alex would take them back when he found out her father was the judge who sent his brother to jail, where he ultimately died.

No. She didn't belong here, didn't deserve to be with Alex, no matter how much she loved him.

She tried to get up, her body still pulsing with pleasure, but he held on to her arm.

"Wait a minute, what's wrong?"

"I need to go. Right now," she said, wresting her arm away from his grasp and stood up. Scrabble pieces and rose petals littered the floor around her.

"Wait a minute. Why?"

She heard in his voice how hurt he was, and she hated herself for doing this to him…again.

Without looking at him, she pulled her dress around her, walked into the kitchen and grabbed her things.

"Hey!" He jumped off the table after her. "Talk to me."

"There are things about me you don't know, Alex," she cried, as she yanked her coat from the closet. "Things you wouldn't like."

"Nonsense, I know all I need to know. I love you."

He grabbed her arm, but she shook away from his grasp.

"Love is not enough. It never is, don't you realize that?" she shouted. "My job here is done. I can't help you anymore, Alex. It hurts too much."

And with that, she pulled the door open and walked out of his life. The knowledge that she was leaving him broken and hurting because of her own cowardice would haunt her forever.

Chapter 13

The morning after Cara walked out on him, Alex sat in his favorite booth at the Tick Tock Diner, clutching his second cup of coffee. His head pounded like he'd been sucker-punched by a made-for-TV wrestler, but his mind was absolutely clear.

Somehow, someway, he was going to find out where Cara lived and demand that they talk through the problems he hadn't even known they had. He rubbed the heel of his hand against his temple. Why were men always the last to know these things?

She'd mentioned that there were things he didn't know about her. He sucked in a breath. Well, there were some things she didn't know about him either, so they had that in common.

It was time to set the record straight.

But the truth was he didn't want to upset her even more than he already had. Their incredible evening of lovemaking had left him wanting even more of her. The fact that the night had ended so badly made his heart ache. He just hoped he hadn't lost her forever.

Alex was on his third cup when Tommy arrived, wearing his trademark Kangol hat. The waitress came over immediately with a cup of coffee and took their orders. They each had the same meal every time; a tall stack of pancakes with bacon and sausage, and a bowl of grits on the side.

Alex pointed to Tommy's head. "It's a red day, huh?" The man owned Kangol hats in every color of the rainbow, and every morning he chose the color based on his mood.

"Yeah, because I'm hopping mad, that's why!" he grumbled as he stirred sugar into his coffee. "I lost three grand to Big Daddy last night. That boy plays poker like he's on the combat line of a war zone."

"I thought you were going to stop going to Big Daddy's poker nights?"

Tommy gulped his coffee, then pointed a finger at him. "Alex, there are two things I'll never give up. Women and cards."

Alex laughed. "It seems I never have any luck with either, so I better stay away from both."

Just then, the waitress brought their breakfast to the table. The two men dug into their food, wolfing it down in silence. When they had finished, they pushed their plates to the side. Now that their bellies were full, it was time to talk business.

"Speaking of women, how are things with Miss Williams?"

Alex shrugged and idly stirred his coffee. "Why do you ask?"

"Are you ready for the book tour?"

He nodded. "I think so."

Tommy leaned his elbows on the table. "You better be," he warned. "Because I just heard you've been doing more than just reading with her. That's the reason I was late."

Alex stopped stirring. "What are you talking about?"

"Cozying up to the little lady at Idella's. Bringing her to the Hideaway. Plus, to make matters worse, you were seen coming out of Beacon House with her."

He felt his face flush with anger. "Who told you all of this?"

"It doesn't matter." Tommy looked around and lowered his gravelly voice. "You were the one who wanted to keep your illiteracy a secret."

Alex clamped his mouth in a thin line, knowing Tommy was right. His heart thudded in his chest. "How bad is it?"

"Don't be surprised if something pops up in the press in the next few days. They know who she is and what she does for a living. It's only a matter of time before they put two and two together. And even if they don't know for sure, they'll report it anyway," Tommy replied, his face grim. "I'll have to say this, she's about the prettiest one you've had the pleasure of introducing to New York City via the headlines in a long time."

Alex threw his arm over his head and slumped down in the booth. "What am I going to do? I can't let the press get to her. It could destroy her. She's not like the others."

"Are you in love with this woman?"

When Alex looked away and didn't reply, Tommy grinned and slapped his knee. "Hot damn. I never thought I'd see the day when Alex Dovington fell head-over-heels in love."

Alex scowled and gulped down his lukewarm coffee. "Look, even if I am, it doesn't matter. She hates me."

"Why?"

"That's just it. I don't know. There's something she's not telling me."

"A woman always has some kind of secret. That's what makes them so intriguing. Besides, you're no saint, either."

"I know, but why couldn't she just tell me, instead of running away?" *And breaking my heart.*

"Probably because she wasn't sure how you'd react. The question you have to ask yourself is, do you want to know what this secret is, and if so, when you find out, are you willing to stick by her, no matter what?"

Alex steepled his fingers. "I think so."

Tommy tipped his hat back, then leaned in and pointed at him. "Think so?" he snorted. "You gotta *know* so. You gotta be so sure about her that nothing will stand in the way of how you feel about this woman. Otherwise, it's all smoke. You dig?"

Alex nodded and smoothed his hand over his head. He got what Tommy was saying, and it was valuable advice. But it was also extremely risky. He'd told her he loved her, for God's sake. And he did.

But who knew what she was hiding beneath her beautiful face? It must be big for her to run out on him like that. He was never one to take chances. What kind of man would gamble his entire future on a woman?

One who wants to be accepted for who he is, despite his past mistakes.

He was that man, and he realized it was time to come clean with everyone, including Cara.

"Can you get me some time with Mo today?"

"I can give it my best shot, why?"

"I need to tell him about my illiteracy before someone else does."

"Great idea!" Tommy paused while the waitress topped off their cups. "What about Cara?"

Alex rubbed his chin. "I love her, T. I've never felt this strongly about someone in my life. And if she's willing to take a chance on me, I'm willing to do the same."

"Great. Why don't you roll by Beacon House this morning and tell her? Bring her some flowers. Women can't resist them."

Alex's mind flashed back to the evening before. When he made love to Cara, the pink and red rose petals had resembled velvety coins on her nude body. He would never be able to look at those flowers again without thinking about her.

He shook his head. "I can't go there. She wouldn't talk to me anyway. I would visit her at home, but I don't know where she lives."

Tommy laughed. "Why didn't you say so? I know where she lives!"

Alex's eyes opened wide with astonishment. "You do? Where?"

"When we were discussing the contract, she told me she lives in Brooklyn. In fact, she lives right next door to my old pal John Sutton. He takes care of her cat whenever she's away. I think the cat's name starts with an M?"

"Molly."

"That's it." Tommy wrote Cara's address on a napkin and handed it to him. Then he took off his hat and laid it on the table. As if on cue, the waitress came over with the bill.

Outside, the two men pumped hands.

"I'll call you as soon as I set up the meeting with Mo."

"What's going to happen after the book tour? Are you going to continue with reading lessons?"

Alex smiled. "If everything goes well tonight, I have more than reading lessons planned for my future."

Tommy chuckled, waved goodbye and shuffled away.

As Alex headed downtown to Parkside Studios, he knew he'd need more than just luck to get Cara back into his life. Like the cowardly lion, he needed courage.

Cara trudged up the stairs to her Brooklyn town house. Between dealing with insensitive creditors and guilt over the pain she'd caused Alex, this was one of the worst days in her life.

She didn't want to think, didn't want to feel. All she wanted was a hot bath and a very large glass of wine.

With a scowl, she dumped her briefcase and purse on the living room couch.

To top it off, the meeting with her lawyer had not gone well. Her landlord planned on renovating the entire space to attract big-box retailers. The paperwork was in order. Unless a miracle happened and somebody purchased the building, there was nothing he could do to stop the eviction.

She kicked off her shoes and hung up her coat, wishing she could disappear into the depths of her closet. Starting tomorrow, she'd have to hold off on accepting any new students.

It pained her to think of saying no to anyone who wanted to learn how to read. But what choice did she have? She didn't want to accept them, then have to turn around and find them placement in other literacy centers. It was better to cut the cord now, before it was too late.

Her mind troubled, she entered the kitchen and selected a bottle of wine from her collection. As she poured herself a large glass, Molly curled a figure eight around her ankles.

Cara had walked out on the sexiest man alive and was losing the business she'd built from the ground up, but at least she still had her beloved cat.

"You love me, don't you?" she asked optimistically.

But before she could reach down to scratch Molly on the top of her head, her cat walked over to her bowl and meowed.

"Oh, I see how you are," she scolded. "You only love me because I'm the one that feeds you. I get it."

It was pathetic, but her spirits were so low that even her cat's rejection hurt her feelings.

As she fed Molly, her thoughts turned to Alex. After her little drama session last night, she didn't expect to hear from him ever again. She only hoped that it wouldn't affect his performance at the book tour on Friday.

She clapped a hand to her forehead when she realized she might not even receive the donation from him. Even though he was legally bound to pay her, she wasn't sure he would. And she couldn't blame him after the way she acted last night.

Her heart pounded in her chest. She was just an ordinary woman who just happened to love, and be loved by, an extraordinary man. She still could not believe all that had transpired between them.

But by walking out on him last night, she'd missed her only opportunity to express her feelings. Now he would never know how much she loved him, too.

Her eyes swam with tears. The best thing she could do now was to concentrate on saving Beacon House—

on her own. It had been a mistake from the very beginning to count on anyone but herself.

She was on her way upstairs when the doorbell rang.
She peeked through the peephole and frowned. Plas-
tering a cheerful smile on her face, she pulled the door
open.

"Hi, Daddy."

Uh-oh, she thought when he didn't reply as he
shrugged off his coat and hung it up in the closet. She
wondered what the lecture topic would be this time.

"I didn't know you were going to stop by. How are
you?" she inquired as they walked into the living room.

They both sat on the couch with rigid spines and
faces that masked their true feelings.

"Cara, I'm fine. But some pretty disturbing news
about you has come to my attention."

Her heart dropped. "What is it?"

"How could you have allowed yourself to get into a
situation where you're threatened with eviction?"

She sucked in a breath. "How did you find out?"

"I'm a judge. I work in the New York City judicial
system. People tell me things. They know you're my
daughter. Besides it's the only way I ever find out anything about you. You never talk to me."

"I never tell you anything because you never listen,"
she retorted, hating the bitter tone in her voice.

"I'm listening now, and I want to help."

"You want to help?" she snorted and folded her arms.
"Why now? I would think you would *want* me to fail.
You're the one who pressured me to go to law school,
and when I chose to become a teacher, you never let
me forget it."

"I wanted you to become a lawyer because I knew

that the life of a teacher would be difficult, and I didn't want that for you."

She slapped her hands against her thighs in exasperation and rose from her seat.

"But what about what I wanted, Daddy?" Her voice rose. "I wanted a father who was there while I was a kid. Who cared more about me than his political career.

"Did I get it?" she railed. "And now, you have the nerve to come in here and try to rescue me? From something that is absolutely none of your business? If you haven't noticed, I'm an adult now. I. Don't. Need. You!"

Her words hung suspended in the air, but the hurt look on her father's face made her wish she could snatch them back into her mouth.

"I'm not going anywhere until we talk about this," said her father sternly. Then he softened his voice. "I know I wasn't around when you were smaller, especially after your mother passed away. And I'm sorry, but there's nothing I can do to change the past."

He stood and went over to her. "But what I can do is be there now. I've been hearing great things about you, Cara. A lot of the people who've been in my courtroom tell me they've been through your literacy program. And even though they may have temporarily fallen back into crime or drugs, they've told me that you're the one person who really cared about them and gave them hope.

"Beacon House is an important community organization in Harlem, but more than that, it's your brainchild and your dream. You're my daughter, I'm proud of you and I want to help you save it."

This was the first time her father told her he was proud of her. She burst out crying and buried her hands in her face to hide her tears. The moment was bittersweet. Perhaps there was a chance that they could reconcile and she could have the kind of relationship with her father that she'd always wanted.

"Daddy, I don't know what to do," she cried. "I'm going to lose Beacon House." The faces of her students flashed by in her mind. "My clients, where will they go?" she sobbed. "I've worked so hard…"

His arms closed around her, strong and safe, and she cried on his shoulder. "Don't worry. We'll find a way."

The doorbell rang again. "Are you expecting anyone?" her father asked.

Cara shook her head, wiping the tears away from her eyes and nose.

"I'll be back in a minute. Wait here."

When she opened the door, her heart seized with panic.

Alex.

Oh, God, what if he saw her father? She had to get him out of here right away.

"Hi, Cara," he said, his voice low and apologetic. "Mind if I come in?"

Before she could answer, he strode through the door like he owned the place. She was relieved when he didn't venture into the hallway but stopped just outside the small foyer.

She closed the door behind them, turned and crossed her arms. "How did you find me?" she demanded in a low whisper.

"Tommy gave me your address," he said in an offhand manner.

His eyes widened and she felt heat rise to her cheeks.

"You've been crying. What's wrong?" he asked, staring at her tear-stained face.

"Nothing." She wiped the tears away and took a step

forward. Being close to him made her knees tremble, but going to another area of the house was out of the question.

"What are you doing here?"

He winced. He didn't know that her sharp tone wasn't meant to hurt him, but she had to get him out of the house before her father saw them.

"We need to talk about last night."

He tried to embrace her, but she pushed him away and strode back to the foyer. "There's nothing more to talk about, Alex." She placed her hand on the doorknob. "Listen, I'm extremely busy and I'm asking you to leave. Now."

He ran his hand over his head, and she could see on his face that he was struggling to maintain composure.

He gave her a confused look. "What's going on with you, Cara?"

"Nothing's going on," she lied. "I just want to be left alone."

"That's not the impression I got last night when I was making love to you."

She kept her voice calm, and although she knew her next words were a lie, she had to hurt him in order to get him out of her life forever.

"That was a mistake."

He pressed his lips together, his laser-intense gaze boring a hole right into her heart. "You don't mean that."

She lifted her chin, forcing herself to look him straight in the eyes. "Yes, I do, Alex," she insisted. "You're a wonderful, charming man. But it would never work between us. We're too different. I'm too…"

"Afraid?" he cut in, raising an eyebrow. "Isn't that it? Everything we shared at my cottage and last night, my love for you, scares the hell out of you, doesn't it? Why don't you just admit it?"

Her stomach knotted and she winced from the pain. He was right, but she wasn't going to tell him that. It was too late.

She lowered her voice, trying desperately to maintain control over her emotions. "I fulfilled my end of the contract. I taught you to read, enough so you'll be able to complete the book tour. There's no reason for us to see each other ever again."

He nodded, and took a step closer. "Yeah, you taught me how to read, but you forgot one thing."

She narrowed her eyes and pressed her back to the door. "What are you talking about?"

"You weren't supposed to teach me how to fall in love with you and then walk out of my life. I don't think that was part of the deal, was it?"

Oh, Lord, her heart felt like it was being cut into slivers. To know he was hurting, because of her.

It hurt so bad to have this conversation with him, to keep her voice hard and unfeeling and her demeanor tough on the outside. All so he wouldn't think she loved him or needed him, when the opposite was true.

She shrugged. "I can't control how you feel about me."

His shoulders recoiled and he glared at her. "Do you treat all your clients like this?" His voice dripped with sarcasm. "Or just the ones you screw?"

Tears sprang to her eyes. She felt like he'd slapped her and at that moment, she wished she'd never laid eyes on him. Her face burned with anger at this arrogant and self-righteous man. How dare he say something so vile?

"Who do you think you are?" she shouted, her brain so overloaded with pain and despair that she forgot where she was. "You don't know me at all, and you never will."

She abruptly turned her back on him and opened the door. "Get out!" she screamed.

He hung his head, then walked toward her and slammed the door shut so hard the hinges rattled.

He drew in close to her, and placed his palm on the door, and his other hand on the wall. "I'm not going anywhere."

"Yes, you are, young man."

The tone of her father's voice was as powerful as the gavel he wielded on a daily basis, and Cara squeezed her eyes shut against a sudden wave of nausea. How long had he been standing there listening to their shouting match? She'd been so angry at Alex that she'd completely forgotten her father was in the other room.

Alex scowled, dropped his hand from the door, and stepped away from her. She felt invisible as the two men stared each other down like two lions ready to rumble in the jungle.

"Crawford Williams." Her father extended his hand first. "The *Honorable* Crawford Williams. I don't believe we've met."

When Alex ignored the outstretched hand and peered at her father like his face held an answer, she clenched her fists at the panic that rose in her chest.

Alex shook his head, as if trying to jog his memory. "No, we've never met, but haven't I seen you before?"

Her father stared him down, then shrugged. "I don't know. You tell me. And while you're at it, why don't you tell me why you're disrespecting my daughter."

"Your daughter?" Alex whipped around to look at her, and her veins went icy with fear.

"Cara is my daughter. Do you have a problem with

that, young man? Now, you better start talking…or start walking."

"Daddy, please," she begged. "Let us have a moment to ourselves and we'll get this worked out."

Alex looked up at the ceiling. "Wait a minute." He snapped his fingers so loud that the sound echoed off the foyer's plaster walls.

He turned his attention on her father. "You're Judge Williams."

"I believe that's what I already said, young man." He turned to Cara. "He may be rude, but he's smart," he wisecracked.

"You're the one who gave my twin brother that harsh jail sentence."

Her father held up his hand. "Whoa. My sentence always fits the crime."

"Does the name Michael Dovington ring a bell?"

Her father scratched his beard. "No, I'm afraid not. But then again, thousands of cases hit my bench every year. How do you know I was the judge in your brother's case and not someone else?"

"My mother showed me your picture in the newspaper. She wrote you a letter. She asked you to have mercy on my brother. She called and called, but you never responded. Not even once. He died in jail because of you!"

He shook his head. "Listen, son. I don't remember any letter. And why would I? I probably get hundreds of those every year. They're all the same to me. Desperate measures from desperate people," he scoffed.

"Daddy!" Cara cried out. Although she wasn't surprised at his insensitive comment, she hurt for Alex.

He took a step toward the judge, one hand clenched into a tight fist. "You bastard!"

Cara stepped in between the two men. "Alex, Daddy. Please don't do this!"

He turned toward Cara, his forehead creased in anger. "And you knew the entire time, didn't you? How?"

Her chin quivered and her voice was watery. "When I was a teenager, I saw you and your mom on television talking about the letter she wrote. Then I went upstairs to my father's office and I found it. Unopened."

"My mom was right all along. You never read it," he said, more to himself than to them. "I trusted you, Cara." His voice broke. "I trusted you!"

She put her hand on his arm but he shook it off. "Alex, I wanted to tell you, but…"

"But what? You thought I was too dumb to understand? Well, I may not be able to read *War and Peace,* but I can read the writing on the wall. It says you're a liar, just like your father."

He took an envelope out of his coat, tossed it at her feet. "You don't want to see me again? Well, Daddy's little girl's gonna get her wish." Then he pulled open the door and stalked out.

Tears of shock flowed down Cara's face. Her body wouldn't move, her mind only held one horrible, heartbreaking truth.

He's gone.

Her father picked up the envelope and closed the door. He led her into the living room and handed her a box of tissues.

"I don't know who that young man is, but he is obviously in love with you."

She blew her nose and squinted at him, puffy-eyed. "Daddy, that's Alex Dovington. The famous jazz saxophonist. Don't you recognize him?"

Her father made a face. "The guy that's always in the paper with a different woman hanging on his arm like a Christmas ornament?"

Cara giggled, in spite of her sadness. "That's him."

"I don't recall the case."

"His brother was a gang member, and I guess his mom always thought he was innocent of the crime."

Her father rolled his eyes. "All mothers think their sons are innocent, even when the evidence proves that they're not." He sighed. "Maybe that's for the best. Gives these boys some hope, even when they don't stand a chance."

He cast a curious glance at the envelope. "He seems pretty taken with you. What's the nature of your relationship?"

"Alex is illiterate. I was hired to teach him how to read within a very short time frame, in exchange for a donation to Beacon House. I should have told him the truth from the very beginning, but there never seemed to be a right time."

She ran her hands down her face, smearing her makeup even more. "I didn't want to lie to him, but God help me, I didn't want to lose his donation."

"And now you're afraid you won't get it?"

She shrugged. "We have a contract, but I'm not sure if he'll live up to it."

"Well, if he doesn't pay you, let me know. I know a couple of lawyers who'd be glad to take your case."

"That won't be necessary. Besides, it doesn't matter now. Whether he sends it to me or not, it will never be enough to save Beacon House."

"Don't give up yet," he chided gently. "I can't help you with your love life, but at least I can do this." He rose to leave.

"Thanks, Daddy."

After they said goodbye, she took the envelope into the kitchen and eyed it suspiciously. When she opened it, she discovered a CD inside with no label on it, and she popped it into the player. Her mouth dropped open when she heard her own voice through the speakers.

It was a fully produced recording of her singing his ballad. Alex must have mixed in the piano, bass and drums, as well as himself on saxophone, after she'd left the studio.

She began to cry uncontrollably as she listened to her sing words she'd written herself:

I can't understand
Why you ever
Left me
Now is the time for you and me
To take a chance on love

And as the song began to fade and Alex played the last note, she crumpled to the floor and sobbed, "Now is the time to say goodbye."

Chapter 14

Alex propped *The Jungle Trumpeteer* on the music stand and opened it to the first page. He attached his saxophone to his lariat, made sure he was comfortably seated, then played a couple of blues scales to relax. His travel coffee mug was on the floor next to him, plus a cold bottle of Pellégrino.

Everything was in place. There were less than twenty-four hours before the start of the tour and he was ready to review the book. Yet there was one thing missing.

Cara.

His heart was filled with regret over the fight they'd had last night. He wished he could take back all the awful things he'd said to her. He could see on her face how much his words had hurt her, something he never wanted to do.

He hadn't come to her home to fight, but to make

up. To tell her again that he loved her, that he couldn't live without her.

She sure was right about one thing. He really didn't know her at all.

Had he fallen in love with a fantasy?

He clamped his eyes shut and her beautiful face, one he would never tire of adoring, floated through his mind.

Why did she have to lie to him? Why couldn't she have just told him the truth from the very beginning?

If she had, would you have still fallen in love with her?

Alex's eyes flew open, and he hung his head because he knew the answer was no.

If he had found out that the Honorable Crawford Williams was Cara's father, she wouldn't have made it past his doorstep, let alone into his bed. He would have done anything he possibly could to get out of the contract and the book tour. He'd even have risked increasing Mo's displeasure with him.

Instead, he'd been played for a fool. And now his career could be over anyway.

This afternoon, he was scheduled to meet with Mo. He planned to tell the hard-nosed owner of Sharp Five Records about his illiteracy, before he read it in Friday's paper. And if he knew Mo as well as he thought he did, the man would not be happy. When he walked out of Mo's office, he wasn't even sure he'd still be a part of the artist roster.

At this point, he didn't care.

Meeting Cara's father last night was horrible enough. He came face-to-face with his own guilt and he knew he'd never be the same person again. He'd blamed Judge Williams for Michael's death for so long that he'd come to believe it himself.

Yet he was the one responsible.

He ran a hand over his head, remembering the night when his life had changed forever. He'd just gotten off the train from playing a gig uptown, and the leader of the BJD (Brooklyn J-Dawgz), the local gang at the time, was waiting for him with his hand out as usual. He held a knife to his neck when Alex wouldn't give them his gig money. Then he took his saxophone and threw it down onto the tracks, and a few seconds later, the train crushed it.

Alex closed his hand into a fist in anger at the memory. "What are you gonna do now, bro?" the leader had said. "How you gonna earn me some money? I guess you gotta steal one now." The he pressed the tip of his knife into Alex's neck, drawing blood.

Michael was with him that night. He said he would steal the saxophone, and took Alex's place in the gang, so that Alex could continue to make music and money for their family.

Alex hugged the stolen saxophone to his chest and buried his face in his hands. The last time he'd cried was at Michael's funeral. When his brother died, Alex had sealed his heart up so tight no one could get in.

Until he met Cara. Then everything changed. He felt alive when he looked at her sweet face, when he touched her gorgeous body. Her talent, intellect and humor sparked an energy within him that he thought was long dead.

And when they made love, he fit within her deliciously, perfectly. She seemed to be created just for him. He hardened just thinking about their nights together.

God, he missed her.

But there was no way in hell he'd ever try to get her back again.

Since he was a kid, he'd always told himself he'd put his heart on the line only once and if it got tossed back in his face, that was it. He would never take another chance and risk getting hurt again. And he knew in his heart that he would never love another woman like he loved Cara.

But what saddened him the most was that his love for her was only beginning. There were many more feelings and emotions to be explored that would never be experienced.

Alex took a sip of his coffee and gagged. Cold.

He rubbed a hand down his face and took a deep breath. He pulled the music stand closer and began to slowly read aloud. He was on his own now, and he had to make the best of it.

With a sigh, he began to read. Slowly, he spelled and sounded out the letters as Cara had taught him. It was hard, and he had to pause several times and take a breath to quell his frustration.

When the doorbell rang and he jumped up to answer it, hope lodged in his heart.

"It's about time…" His words fell away at the sight of Judge Williams. It took everything in him not to slam the door in his face.

He stared hard at the portly man. "Judge Williams, to what do I owe this unpleasant surprise?"

"May I come in?" His eyes blinked rapidly behind his Malcolm X glasses. "I need to talk to you."

A twinge of fear gripped him. Had something happened to Cara?

With a resigned shrug, he stepped aside so Williams could enter, then shut the door and led the way to the living room.

"Have a seat, *your Honor,*" he said with mock authority.

Judge Williams removed his trench coat, laid it carefully on the arm of the couch and sat down on the leather couch. The cushions whined, but the man didn't seem to notice.

Alex eased into a chair across from him, his face impassive.

Crawford adjusted his glasses. "After you boldly accused me of judicial indiscretion, my curiosity got the best of me. Today, I did a little digging around."

His eyes drifted to his saxophone and Alex felt his stomach plummet. He tightened his grip on the instrument that had been the source of so much joy and pain over the years. How had he let things get this far?

Crawford regarded him a moment. "I may have judged your brother too harshly. The BJD were getting too bold with their criminal activity. They needed to be stopped."

"So what are you trying to say? That you needed my brother to be an example?"

"It wasn't just him, but something like that."

"Michael's dead. He can't be an example to anyone, so, what's your point?"

"You know, Alex, the mind can be the worst jail cell on earth for a brother struggling to forget the mistakes he made in the past. Don't make Cara suffer because you're still struggling to break free."

Alex's heart dropped into his stomach. Everything the judge said made sense. Letter or no letter, although he had no one to blame for Michael's death but himself, maybe it was time to let go of the pain and the guilt that had haunted him for years.

Crawford rose to leave, laying his coat over his arm. "I'm due back in court, not that I'm in any hurry to get there."

Alex escorted him to the door. "Why's that?"

"Son, I've got a double homicide case waiting for me. My fourth this month." Crawford shook his head, blew out a harsh breath. "New York. The city where killers never sleep."

Alex opened the door and the judge walked out without another word.

"Judge Williams," he called out. "Why *did* you come here and tell me all that?"

He turned on his heel and looked at Alex. "Because I love my daughter, and I think you do, too." Then he hailed a cab and sped away.

He's right.

Ever since he'd met Cara, there wasn't a moment when she wasn't on his mind. She was part of his dreams, his very being, and his desire for her had only grown stronger and more powerful the longer he was away from her.

Clearly, she did not feel the same way. So if he could only love her from afar, that's what he would do. He would go on with his own life, but he would love her. No one else. It was as simple as that.

As he gathered up his saxophone and other things he needed for his tell-all meeting with Mo, his mind was formulating a plan. It was a long shot, but if it worked it would fix everything and show his love for Cara at the same time.

Although he wasn't a religious man, his lips moved in a silent prayer for hope, redemption and second chances.

* * *

Cara slammed the phone down and cradled her fore-head in her palms, another no clanging in her ears like a church bell. Every moment of the last twenty-four hours had been more miserable than the last. It took everything in her to lift up the phone to plead for help. After a morning of rejections, things were not looking good.

She didn't know how much more of this she could take.

In just under a week, her life had drastically changed. She'd fallen in love, lost her man and was on the verge of losing her business. In the time it took God to create the whole world, she'd managed to nearly destroy everything she'd ever worked for in her own life.

She stretched her hands above her head and yawned, then flopped her head back on her arms like a rag doll. She'd been up half the night crying and listening to the CD he'd given her over and over.

Alex had given her his heart, told her that he loved her. But he probably hated her now. She had betrayed him out of fear, and that was unforgivable.

Her heart wrenched when she thought about him, what she'd lost. She reached up and stroked a single flower in the large arrangement she'd received from Alex yesterday morning. The vase was filled with flowers of many sizes and varieties. She inhaled the scents as she reread the card tied with a red ribbon to a Gerbera daisy.

> I didn't know what flower was your favorite, so I bought one of each. I can't wait for our next game of Scrabble. I love you.
> Alex

She shook her head. While he was choosing the flowers, he'd probably never imagined that he would discover that she was hiding a secret that would ultimately end any feelings he had for her.

Nancy's voice, patched through the intercom, broke through her thoughts.

"Cara, I'm sorry to disturb you, but you have a visitor."

"What? I thought you canceled all of my appointments for today."

"I did." Nancy's voice dropped to a whisper. "But this man insists on seeing you."

"Who is it?"

"Tommy Jenkins. Do you know him?"

Her heart sank. "Yes, send him in."

A minute later, Cara greeted Tommy warmly at the door. "It's great to finally meet you in person."

His hand felt old and rough on her palm and his smile held the glow of a child on Christmas morning. She felt herself smiling back when she wanted to do nothing but cry.

Tommy hung up his coat and sat down. "Beautiful flowers. Looks like a rainbow exploded. I can appreciate color." He pointed to his bright yellow hat. "I've got one for every mood."

She chuckled. "Oh? What mood are you in today?"

"Thankful. And I think you'll feel the same in due time. How did things go with Alex?"

"You haven't spoken with him?"

"I have, but I want to hear from you."

"Things were difficult at first," she admitted. "Alex put up plenty of roadblocks, but then he relaxed and learned to trust me. After that point, it got much easier to teach him."

"Well, when I spoke to him, he had nothing but compliments about you."

She frowned. "That's surprising."

"Why is that?"

She bit her lip in hesitation. "We didn't part on the best of terms."

"Alex is lucky to have you as a teacher."

"Thank you. Based on the circumstances, I think I've taken him as far as I can. Before you leave, I'll give you a list of other literacy centers he can contact for lessons."

Tommy removed his hat and scratched his head. "Why shouldn't he come here to continue learning to read?"

A lump lodged in her throat. "We've had differences that I believe would impede the learning process. Besides, having a lesson here is not going to be possible—for anyone."

"Why is that?"

She took a deep breath and spoke quietly. "Beacon House will be closing by the end of the month." Even saying the words, she could hardly believe them.

The smile disappeared from Tommy's face. "I'm sorry to hear that. What happened?"

"Too much to talk about, but I am really hoping he'll continue with reading lessons. He's come a long way, but he's got a long way to go."

Tommy pulled an envelope from the front pocket of his shirt. "Maybe this will help?"

Cara accepted and opened the envelope. Her heart leapt, than quickly sank, leaving her dazed. Inside was the donation for her services. It would help maintain payroll and keep the lights on through the end of the month, but not much else.

"Thank you. This is exactly what we agreed to, but I'm afraid it's not enough to keep our doors open."

"I'm sorry to hear that. I'll let Alex know."

"No, don't!"

Tommy raised his eyebrows and she realized she'd spoken a little louder than she intended.

"I'm sorry. It's just that this is a private matter that I wish to handle on my own."

"Birds of a feather," muttered Tommy.

"Excuse me?"

"I don't know you very well, but you're as hard-headed as he is. Both too stubborn to ask for help when you know you really need it, and both too proud to admit you can't live without one another."

"Tommy," she replied. "With all due respect, you don't know me, nor do you know the situation, so you really shouldn't judge me."

He waved her comment away. "I call 'em as I see 'em, just like when I play poker. Only this time, I got a winning hand. I don't even have to look at it to know that you're in love with Alex."

Her eyes welled up with tears as she stared at him in disbelief. Why did her feelings for Alex make sense when they came from someone else's lips, but on her own they only confused her?

"Yes, I am. But that doesn't matter anymore."

"What are you talking about, it doesn't matter—of course it matters. Why, my Dora and I have been married over twenty-five years and you don't think we've had our little spells? But no matter how much she made me angry or hurt me, I still loved her, and she still loved me. Because when a man loves a woman, really loves her, he'll let nothing stand in his way."

Cara snorted. "I guess that answers my question. You don't see Alex around here, do you?"

"There's one thing that marriage has taught me. Sometimes you have to be the one to forgive first. Come to the book reading tomorrow."

"I can't."

"Can't or won't?" countered Tommy.

"He wouldn't want me there. It would only make things worse. This is an important day for him."

Tommy stood up, grabbed his coat and adjusted his hat. "All the more reason for the woman he loves to be there.

"Just think about it."

He shut the door behind him, leaving Cara alone. She squeezed back her tears and accepted the truth.

Alone.

It was exactly what she deserved to be.

Chapter 15

Cara's heels resounded with a confidence she really didn't feel as she walked down the hallway of PS 25. The walls were lined with children's artwork depicting classic elements of the fall season. When she reached the office, Mrs. Esther Dawson, principal of PS 25, greeted her warmly.

"Cara!" she exclaimed, hugging her. "It's so good to see you again."

"It's great to be here, Mrs. Dawson," she replied, hugging her back.

She smiled at the older woman, who stood not much taller than her own five feet and whose moniker was "The Destroyer." But in her case, it wasn't a negative term. She was well-known in New York City for turning some of the worst elementary schools in the system into the best.

"Let's go into my office," she said. "Would you like some coffee?"

Cara declined the offer and had a seat at the little round conference table.

"Did you see the news truck outside?"

Cara nodded and sat up straighter in her chair. "Yes, a crew from NY One."

Mrs. Dawson grinned. "They just arrived. There are other reporters that are supposed to be coming, too. *New York Post*, *New York Daily News*, *New York Times,* even *Entertainment Weekly*."

"Wow, that's wonderful. Did Mr. Dovington arrange it?"

Mrs. Dawson shook her head. "No, everything was arranged by his record company," she replied. "They shared their media plan with me and everyone that will be present today met my approval. Literacy is a message that everyone in New York and across the country needs to hear. Don't you agree?"

Cara nodded, but her heart went out to Alex, whom she was sure did not want to be the poster child. Was he aware that he was walking into a trap?

"I was surprised and pleased to hear from you yesterday," Mrs. Dawson continued. "The children are so excited about Alex visiting the school, and you being here will make the event that much more special."

Cara smiled. "I always enjoy coming and reading to the kids, especially the younger ones."

"You and Beacon House are a vital part of the Harlem community," agreed Mrs. Dawson. "I don't know what we would do without you! Will you be reading with Mr. Dovington?"

"Oh, no," she interrupted. "In fact, I have a favor to ask."

Mrs. Dawson raised an eyebrow. "What can I do for you?"

"I know this is an unusual request, but I'd rather Alex not know I was here."

"It's none of my business, but can I ask why?"

"My reasons for being here are primarily personal, so I can't really go into it."

"I understand. But the children will be so disappointed. Can't I even announce that you're here?"

"Of course. But I prefer that you do so after you announce Alex. Is that all right?"

"It is unusual, but I'm happy to accommodate you. Can I assume you don't want him to see you, either?"

She nodded. "Is there someplace I can hang out until the event starts?"

Mrs. Dawson nodded and checked her watch. "Alex's publicist said he'd be arriving around 8:30 a.m., so we'd better hurry. Come with me, I have somewhere you can hide."

They exited the office and walked down a sloping hallway to the auditorium. But instead of turning and entering the doors, they went a little farther, and Mrs. Dawson led her backstage.

They stopped in front of a small room lit by a single bulb.

"This is where we keep all the props when we're doing a play. We haven't done one in about a year, so the room is a little dusty, but it will have to do. You should be able to hear me announce your name from the stage."

"This is perfect. Thank you, Mrs. Dawson."

She nodded. "Just remember to turn off the light before you leave."

Mrs. Dawson started to close the door, but then turned to Cara. "I don't know why you're doing all this, but I hope everything turns out the way you want it."

"Me, too," Cara whispered as the door shut.

She backed into the room and jumped when her legs brushed against something rough. As her eyes adjusted to the dim light, she discovered that it was just a stack of old carpeting. She found a wooden chair in a corner, brought it closer to the light and sat down.

She took her phone from her purse and silenced it. A few minutes later, her hand flew to her throat. Alex's rich baritone voice rang through the auditorium as he tested the microphone he really didn't need.

Closing her eyes, she longed to hear his voice against her earlobe, a lover's whisper. Warmth pooled in her belly as she thought about the other evening with Alex in his dining room.

The night he told her he loved her and made love to her with such unforgettable passion.

It was one of the most wonderful nights of her life, and she had ruined it by running away from him. Being with him had been a dream come true, but it was time to wake up to reality. She'd be lucky if he ever spoke to her again.

She opened her eyes and stood. Her hand hovered over the doorknob for a second before she twisted it and cracked open the door.

The stage curtain, a bloodred velvet, partially blocked her view as she peeked through, but there was a tiny opening and she could see that Alex's back was to her.

He was walking back to the podium on the other side of the stage playing a funked-up version of the Rolling Stone's tune "Start Me Up." She could barely tear her eyes away as his body moved ever so slightly in time with the music. She found herself tapping her feet until he suddenly turned and started walking in her direction.

She shut the door and leaned against it, hoping he

hadn't seen her. Her heart was beating so fast that it felt like it was going to thump right out of her chest. He'd stopped playing and she could hear his hard-soled shoes on the wooden floor, walking toward the prop room.

She slowly locked the door a moment before Alex turned the outside knob. Cara held her breath as he jiggled it a few times before giving up. When his footsteps faded away, she exhaled in relief and sat down in the chair.

Maybe hiding in here wasn't such a good idea, she thought, as she realized that until Mrs. Dawson announced him, Alex would probably be waiting backstage, too. She'd have to be extra quiet to avoid being heard. Thankfully, the event would be starting soon.

She jumped in her seat when something hard banged against the door. Tiptoeing toward it, she put her ear against the door.

"Mr. Dovington, is everything okay?" said a voice.

"Everything is fine. I'm just hanging out here until we get started."

"Can I get you some water?"

"Sure, if you could just place it by the podium that would be great."

"No problem, Mr. Dovington, and good luck!"

Her heart wrenched in her chest when he gave no response, just a sigh so deep it rumbled against the door.

He must be so nervous right now, she thought, remembering how terrified he was that his secret would someday be exposed. If only there was something she could do to help him relax.

Carefully, she placed her palms flat against the door, where she thought his shoulders might be leaning. Next, she inched her feet forward until her breasts were grazing the surface. Finally, she pressed her cheek against the door and closed her eyes.

She imagined her arms coming from behind and enclosing him in a surprise hug, her breasts and tummy pressed against the hard muscles of his back. In her mind, she planted a kiss on his shoulder and squeezed him so tight it was like she would never let him go.

When she stepped away from the door a few minutes later, tears were streaming down her face. She twisted a finger around one of her curls, dreading what was to come. For the millionth time, her mind ran through what she would say to Alex.

But there's no easy way to say goodbye.

Although the media coverage was an annoyance, perhaps it wasn't all bad. At least he couldn't throw her out on national TV, she mused sadly.

She was blotting her tears with a tissue, trying to salvage her makeup, when she heard what sounded like hundreds of feet thunder into the auditorium. The children themselves were surprisingly quiet, although she heard the occasional snicker that was quickly followed by multiple rounds of "shhhs."

Even though she was backstage behind closed doors, the hum of excitement in the air was palpable.

"We're ready to get started," announced Mrs. Dawson. "You should all be on voice meter one, which if you are still trying to wake up, means that there should not be one sound coming out of your mouths."

There was a pause while she waited, presumably for everyone to be quiet.

"Students and faculty of PS 25, we have the honor today of being the first school on a city-wide literacy tour conducted by Alex Dovington, world-famous saxophonist."

"Mr. Dovington has nine albums to his credit, one of which won a Grammy Award, the highest honor in the music industry. He is also an alumnus of PS 25 and he had his first jazz performance right on this very stage. Everyone put your hands together now for Mr. Alex Dovington!"

As the auditorium erupted in applause, Cara heard Alex push away from the door and start playing a popular hip-hop tune as he walked onstage. The roar of sound as the kids hooped, hollered and stomped their feet along with the music was amazing to hear.

Cara opened the door and peeked out. After a wailing high note that made the crowd go wild, he walked over to the podium and thanked the audience. A smattering of flashbulbs went off.

"Oh, I nearly forgot," exclaimed Mrs. Dawson, standing at his side. "Excuse me, Alex."

After reclaiming the microphone, she announced, "Children, we have a surprise guest with us this morning. Many of you know her as an educator who has volunteered countless hours in the classroom."

"But you may not know that she is also the author of several books for children and young adults, including the one Alex will be sharing with us today."

"Please welcome to the stage, Miss Cara Williams!"

Even though she was expecting the announcement, her mouth went dry when she heard her name. Her feet felt rooted to the floor. Her hands shook as she opened the door and walked out of the prop room.

She pushed the back of her hand against the red velvet curtain. Her eyes locked with Alex's, and she could see that he was stunned to see her.

The applause made her knees jittery and her heart

beat faster as he started walking toward her from the other end of the stage, his eyes never leaving her face.

And she couldn't take her eyes off him. His navy blue button-down shirt and black dress pants barely contained his sexual magnetism. It lit her body on fire in such a way that made her blush under the hot stage lights.

He was movie-star beautiful, emanating an aura of confidence and self-assuredness that would fool anyone into thinking he was on top of his game.

Only she knew the truth. He was scared. For better or worse, his whole future was about to change.

They met in the middle and her heart leaped in surprise at the grateful smile on his face.

Alex took her gently by the elbow and leaned in close. The scent of his cologne made her mind flash back to the first time he kissed her, and she felt a rush of desire.

Applause encircled them both, but all she heard was his voice whisper low in her ear.

"Thank you for being here."

He linked his arm with hers as he escorted her to the podium as if she were royalty.

He gave her hand a squeeze before he gently let it go. In that moment, she desperately wanted to grab it back, to capture forever the warmth and protectiveness of his flesh on hers.

Alex stepped up to the microphone and Mrs. Dawson motioned to her to sit on one of the folding chairs near the podium.

He unsnapped his saxophone from his lariat and placed it in his instrument stand. He waited patiently until the applause ended before speaking.

"Thank you, everyone, for the warm welcome. It certainly has been a morning of surprises." Her face heated with embarrassment as he turned and glanced at her.

He turned back to the audience. "And I think we may be in for a few more before we're finished here today. But first, I need you guys to answer a couple of questions. Let's say your parents are out of town and you're free to do whatever you want. How many of you would play video games?"

Almost all of the hands in the room shot up.

"How many of you would watch TV or surf the internet?"

Most of the hands were raised.

"Uh-huh, and how many of you would just be hanging with your crew?"

More than a few hands popped up.

"Okay, so how many of you would sit back and read a book?"

Cara counted about seventy-five kids who raised their hands in a crowd of about three hundred. Those who did raise their hands did so tentatively, like they were ashamed.

"Okay, how many would be doing their homework?"

No one raised their hand and everyone laughed, including Alex.

"When you're a kid, you don't realize how important it is to learn how to read," he said, his tone now more serious. "You'd rather be doing anything else in the world because you may think reading is boring, it's hard, or it's just not cool.

"I used to feel the exact same way. School didn't come easily to me. As a matter of fact, I hated it. Eventually I just gave up. I dropped out in the ninth grade and I never graduated from high school. But something much worse happened." He paused for a few beats. "I never learned to read."

There was a murmur of voices and Cara saw several teachers glance at each other at this strange turn of events. The reporters and news crew at the back of the auditorium were perking up and whispering to each other.

"I'm illiterate. Can anyone tell me what the word *illiterate* means?"

Hands shot up and Alex chose a child near the front of the auditorium.

The kid stood up. "It means you can't read or write."

"You got it. I can't read. Not a menu, a grocery list, street signs, the paper, or even my own website.

"I kept it a secret for years. No one knew. Not my record company who set up this tour. Not even my mother."

He took a deep breath. "Let me tell you all something. Not being able to read all these years has been terrible. There's all this knowledge in the world that I couldn't experience because I can't read. It's like being in a prison. And who kept me behind bars?" He pointed his thumb to his chest. "Me. But last Friday, I started reading lessons with Miss Williams."

He walked over and held out his hand to Cara. She looked up at him, confused. He smiled, and enclosing her hand in his led her to the podium.

His eyes locked with hers. "And even though it's only been a week, being able to read, even just a little bit, has changed my life."

Her heart fluttered in her chest; the sincerity in his voice made her want to weep. She gazed at him. The stage lights made his hazel eyes deepen in color, and it was all she could do not to fly into his arms.

The applause and cheers of the children brought her to her senses, and she remembered the second reason why she was here. To say goodbye to him and never look back.

His good looks and charm were meant to be adored by another woman, not her. Someone who had the time and energy for a relationship. Someone who had their life together, instead of falling apart.

"So, when I read to you today, please be patient. I may stumble and fall and make mistakes, but I'm no longer a prisoner.

"Because I can read, now I am free!"

Alex raised both of their hands up in victory, and the whole auditorium went wild.

The electricity she felt between them was incredible. She was so proud of his courageous act.

"Hey, would you like to hear Miss Williams read with me?"

"Yeahhh…" the kids screamed.

"Hold up, I gotta ask her first."

He leaned in close to her. "Will you read with me?"

"Yes," she whispered.

"Score! She said yes!"

The kids started cheering again until Principal Dawson raised her hands up like Moses dividing the Red Sea in half.

He put his hand over the mike and whispered into her ear. "We're on fire, and we're not even in bed."

Cara stifled a giggle as they both reached to open the book and their fingers brushed against one another.

He cleared his throat, bent toward the microphone and paused. Alex's hand shook a little as he turned to the first page.

Cara's heart seized in her chest when he looked at

her, raw fear in his eyes. She smiled her encouragement, reached out and gave his hand a gentle squeeze. He looked away and rolled his shoulders back.

"The Jungle Trumpeteer." He cleared his throat again. "By Molly Mathers, aka Cara Williams."

Alex turned the page, reached for her hand, and slowly began to read.

"Sam was a very large elephant who loved to pretend…"

Cara's heart burst with pride as she watched him. He pronounced each word slowly but clearly and with much expression.

She looked out at the kids in the audience. Every eye was on Alex and it seemed like they were hanging on his every word, holding their breath and struggling with him when he got stuck, breathing with relief when he pushed through a difficult passage.

She jumped in and read some of the other characters in the book, but only because Alex had asked her to.

And when he said "The End," the auditorium erupted in thunderous applause and cheers.

They both stepped away from the podium and walked to the middle of the stage.

Cara smiled at Alex, put her arms around him and hugged him with delight. He took her hand and squeezed it as they both took a bow.

They both beamed with pleasure from the applause of the kids. Her hand felt warm in his and she felt so complete, so wonderful. She'd never imagined things would go this well.

But in the midst of her joy, sadness dwelled. The happiness was only temporary because the event was almost over and so were her dreams of a life with Alex.

Alex walked back to microphone. "Thanks everyone for being so patient and for not throwing stuff at me," he said with a laugh. "I have one other announcement before I play some music and you get to ask me some questions.

"As I mentioned earlier, Miss Williams has been teaching me how to read for the past week. She runs a nonprofit literacy organization called Beacon House, right here in Harlem. She teaches reading to those who cannot read, and gives hope to lives devastated by illiteracy.

"I am profoundly grateful to Cara and have decided to donate fifty percent of the proceeds from my next album to benefit Beacon House."

Cara shrieked and put her hands to her face. His generosity meant that she could purchase the building, and Beacon House could remain open!

Tears stung her eyes as she hugged him, as the kids hooted and clapped and stamped their feet on the floor.

She opened her mouth to speak, but she could not. Instead, she hugged him tighter and cried openly. Tears flowed down her cheeks, for Beacon House and all of her clients, but most of all for Alex.

Lord, how she loved him. How could she possibly say goodbye to him now?

His generosity took care of her problems with Beacon House. She could no longer use that as an excuse to run away from a relationship with him.

But there were still a multitude of issues that made ending her involvement with Alex the right choice. Issues she wasn't sure could be resolved.

Had he truly forgiven her for hiding the truth about her father?

Alex suddenly leaned into her and said, "We need to talk. Will you wait for me backstage?"

She looked up at him and nodded, feeling hope rise from deep within her. Her mind tried to squash it, but her heart knew that right now it was all she had to hold on to, and this time she wasn't letting go.

Cara felt like her whole future was out signing autographs. As she waited backstage for Alex to return, time seemed suspended. She sat in the prop room, her hands trembling so badly they ached, with one thought looping through her mind.

What happens now?

She'd come to support him and then say goodbye. Both were the right thing to do, but Alex changed everything. His generous donation of future album revenues to Beacon House meant she could no longer use her financial difficulties as an excuse to avoid a relationship with him.

In her heart, she knew the one thing that hadn't changed was her love for him. But she still wasn't sure how he felt about her.

There was a knock on the door and she jumped out of her seat.

"Who is it?"

"Your favorite student," replied Alex, his voice low and sexy. Just hearing it calmed her nerves and excited her senses at the same time.

When she closed the door behind him, he set down his instrument case and pulled her into his arms. Relief and happiness flooded through her body at his touch.

She put her arms around his neck and hugged him. "You did it, Alex!" she exclaimed. "I'm so proud of you."

He tightened his hold around her waist. "*We* did it," he emphasized, hugging her back.

When he released her, she looked up and he was smiling ear to ear. "I couldn't have done any of this without you."

She shook her head and played with his collar, her movements shy and tentative. "You did all the work," she insisted.

"Only because I didn't want to end up in the time-out chair," he flirted. "With my face to the wall, how could I have admired your beauty?"

She blushed and waggled her finger at him. "Luckily you were never bad enough."

"Give me another chance, and I'll be the bad boy you've always dreamed of," he joked, but his voice held a seductive note that stirred her desire.

She laughed and hugged him again, feeling blessed that he seemed as happy as she was.

She stepped back. "You were really brave to admit to the kids that you're illiterate. I'm curious. Why did you decide to do it?"

"I was tired of hiding, Cara. You opened my eyes to a world I want to be a part of. When I finally told the truth about myself, I felt like this huge weight that I've carried around for years was lifted from my shoulders. It was amazing."

"What do you think is going to happen now?"

He shrugged his shoulders. "I'm sure the story will be making the newspapers and gossip sites on the internet. Before I came here, I gave a couple of media interviews, and there will be more talk and more questions. I used to be scared of what would happen, but not now."

"Why?"

"Because I have you in my life again. It means a lot to have you here. When I saw you walk across the stage, I was so happy to see you. What changed your mind?"

"It was the right thing to do and—" She paused.

For so long, she'd been afraid to reveal her feelings for Alex, but something inside her, and the courage he'd just displayed in front of everyone, gave her new strength.

"I missed you," she blurted out.

He reached out, ran a finger along the swell of her cheek. "I missed you, too," he replied. "More than you'll ever know."

She trembled inside at his words. They made all the nights lying awake, thinking of him, worth every tear.

"I still can't believe you're going to donate half of the money from your next album to Beacon House."

He smiled at her. "I talked it over with Mo yesterday and surprisingly, he went for the idea. Besides, I'm thinking after this album that I'm going to go out on my own."

She raised an eyebrow. "What do you mean?"

"I'm thinking about starting my own independent record label and music school."

"Oh, Alex, that's wonderful!" she exclaimed, clapping her hands together.

"Thanks! Yes, it's going to be a combination of a music school, recording studio and record label based right here in Harlem. I want to give back to the community like you have, Cara. You inspire me."

"How can I ever thank you?" she whispered, grateful for the kindness she saw in his hazel eyes.

She held her breath as he slowly bent his head toward hers.

"Like this," he said, brushing his lips against hers in a featherlight kiss so sweet and so gentle that tears sprang anew behind her closed eyes.

She leaned into him as his tongue teased her lips open.

"And this." His kiss became more insistent and her body went limp. But at the same time, she felt energy swell within her body that made her feel like she could dance barefoot all the way to the moon.

"And finally this." His hands massaged her back and traveled up to stroke her curls, sending a thousand tingles down her spine.

They held on to each other, arms entangled, mouths moving together in mutual desire as they both lost themselves in one breathless kiss after another.

"Cara," he murmured against her lips. "I need to tell you something."

"Hmm?" she muttered, not wanting to break the kiss.

"About Michael." He stepped back suddenly. "And about me."

Although he kept her only an arm's length away, she shivered from the loss of close contact with his body.

She wanted to tell him that the past didn't matter. But even in the dim light, she could see his eyes were serious. And she sensed in the abrupt change in his demeanor that his mind was made up.

He walked over to the chair, turned it around and straddled it. "I'm a coward."

She rushed to his defense. "No, you're not. You call what you just did out there, placing your reputation on the line, being a coward?"

He held up a hand. "Let me finish. My brother Michael stole my saxophone to protect me from becoming a gang member and living life on the streets. I've carried this saxophone and the weight of guilt over his death for years."

"I'm sorry, Alex," she said, putting her hand on his arm. "That must be so horrible. It wasn't your fault."

"But it was my fault," he insisted. "I should have

never allowed him to take the fall for me. If it wasn't for me, Michael wouldn't have gone to jail, and he wouldn't have died."

Cara looked at him strangely. "But I thought a genetic heart condition was the official cause of death."

"What?" Alex replied in a stunned voice, and he stood up so fast the chair crashed to the floor. "How do you know this?"

"Idella told me at the restaurant. She said your family had an autopsy conducted to find out why Michael died of a heart attack at such a young age. They discovered he had a rare congenital heart condition that went undetected until it was too late."

He ran his hand over his head. "Why didn't my mom or Idella tell me?" he said, pain in his voice.

"I don't know, Alex," she replied, watching him pace back and forth in the tiny room. "Maybe they wanted to protect you from more grief. Idella said his death hit you hard, and even I can see that you're still affected by it."

He turned and leaned against the door. "All these years, I've blamed myself for Michael's death."

"Alex, you didn't know Michael had a heart condition," she said softly, approaching him. "Look at me." She touched his face. "Why continue to punish yourself over something that happened so long ago? It doesn't bring Michael back. Forgive yourself. Let it go."

His eyes were sorrowful as they gazed upon hers, then his voice broke. "I don't know how."

Gently, she laid her hand upon his chest. "You start by looking into your heart. What do you see?"

He glanced down at her hand in silence, eyes questioning.

"I see a caring and generous man who made a mistake. I see someone who needs a second chance," she insisted gently. "A fresh start."

"You're right." He squeezed his eyes shut. "But I still feel like I should do something to somehow make up for everything I did."

"Hmm," Cara said. "Maybe you could purchase some instruments and donate them to PS 25 or other local schools."

He opened his eyes, put his hands on her shoulders and peered at her with amazement. "That's a great idea!"

He frowned again. "What about Michael? Although he didn't know it at the time, his sacrifice allowed me to become who I am today. I need do to something to honor him."

She thought awhile, then took a deep breath. "I think the best way to preserve his memory is to love someone again."

He smiled, his eyes twinkling with surprise at her suggestion. "Miss Williams, are you applying for the position?"

Cara gave him a shy smile. "Maybe, but to be honest, I'm afraid, because I feel like you haven't forgiven me for lying to you about my father. I wanted to tell you so many times during our time together in the Catskills, but I was afraid of losing you."

He tilted her chin up with the tip of his finger. "I have forgiven you, and you will never lose me. Don't ever forget that."

She'd been waiting so long to hear those words that she almost didn't believe him. But when she searched his eyes, her insides quaked when she saw truth there.

He cupped her face gently in his hands. "I love you, Cara. I know I still have a long way to go and a lot to learn. I need a teacher who can handle me, and a wife who will love me forever. Are you up for the task?"

Her heart felt like it was going to explode from joy, and for a moment she was speechless. After thirteen years of hoping and praying, her dream was finally coming true.

Tears of happiness flowed down her face. "Yes, yes, yes!" she exclaimed. "When do you want me to start?"

"How about right now?" he proposed with a passionate kiss, beginning a journey forever filled with books, music and lots of love.

* * * * *

REQUEST YOUR FREE BOOKS!

2 FREE NOVELS
PLUS 2 FREE GIFTS!

KIMANI™
ROMANCE

Love's ultimate destination!

YES! Please send me 2 FREE Kimani™ Romance novels and my 2 FREE gifts (gifts are worth about $10). After receiving them, if I don't wish to receive any more books, I can return the shipping statement marked "cancel." If I don't cancel, I will receive 4 brand-new novels every month and be billed just $4.94 per book in the U.S. or $5.49 per book in Canada. That's a saving of at least 21% off the cover price. It's quite a bargain! Shipping and handling is just 50¢ per book in the U.S. and 75¢ per book in Canada.* I understand that accepting the 2 free books and gifts places me under no obligation to buy anything. I can always return a shipment and cancel at any time. Even if I never buy another book, the two free books and gifts are mine to keep forever.

168/368 XDN FEJR

Name	(PLEASE PRINT)	

Address		Apt. #

City	State/Prov.	Zip/Postal Code

Signature (if under 18, a parent or guardian must sign)

Mail to the **Reader Service:**
IN U.S.A.: P.O. Box 1867, Buffalo, NY 14240-1867
IN CANADA: P.O. Box 609, Fort Erie, Ontario L2A 5X3

Not valid for current subscribers to Kimani Romance books.

Want to try two free books from another line?
Call 1-800-873-8635 or visit www.ReaderService.com.

* Terms and prices subject to change without notice. Prices do not include applicable taxes. Sales tax applicable in N.Y. Canadian residents will be charged applicable taxes. Offer not valid in Quebec. This offer is limited to one order per household. All orders subject to credit approval. Credit or debit balances in a customer's account(s) may be offset by any other outstanding balance owed by or to the customer. Please allow 4 to 6 weeks for delivery. Offer available while quantities last.

Your Privacy—The Reader Service is committed to protecting your privacy. Our Privacy Policy is available online at www.ReaderService.com or upon request from the Reader Service.

We make a portion of our mailing list available to reputable third parties that offer products we believe may interest you. If you prefer that we not exchange your name with third parties, or if you wish to clarify or modify your communication preferences, please visit us at www.ReaderService.com/consumerchoice or write to us at Reader Service Preference Service, P.O. Box 9062, Buffalo, NY 14269. Include your complete name and address.

KROM11B

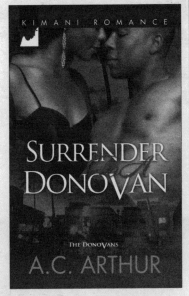

**A brand-new miniseries
featuring fan-favorite authors!**

THE HAMILTONS *Laws of Love*

Family. Justice. Passion.

Ann Christopher	Pamela Yaye	Jacquelin Thomas
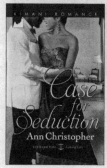	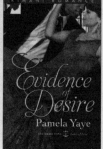	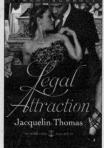
Available September 2012	*Available October 2012*	*Available November 2012*

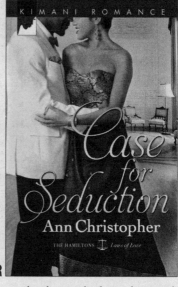 

Harlequin® Desire

ALWAYS POWERFUL, PASSIONATE AND PROVOCATIVE.

A BRAND-NEW WESTMORELAND FAMILY NOVEL FROM *NEW YORK TIMES* BESTSELLING AUTHOR

BRENDA JACKSON

Megan Westmoreland needs answers about her family's past. And Rico Claiborne is the man to find them. But when the truth comes out, Rico offers her a shoulder to lean on...and much, much more. Megan has heard that passions burn hotter in Texas. Now she's ready to find out....

TEXAS WILD

"Jackson's characters are...hot enough to burn the pages."
—*RT Book Reviews* on *Westmoreland's Way*

Available October 2 from Harlequin Desire®.

HD73198K